The Rorschach Montage

Jerome Jones
Jorge Zeledon
Miriam Skerra
Vicki Barrington
Marianne Conlon

Perry Gamsby's

'Become A Published Author'

The Rorschach Montage

Published Major Work
Macarthur Community College, Term 1 2012

Barrington, Vicki. *'The Whiz Kid Of Wall Street'. 'Julia's Story'*
Conlon, Marianne. *'Pete And Mary'*
Jones, Jerome. 'Charlie', *'Road Sweep', 'Mamma San' 'Homecoming'*
Skerra, Miriam. *'Narendra And The Butterfly', 'In the Japanese Garden', 'Intercity Express', 'Flash Fiction'*
Zeledon, Jorge. *'Hola Zorro!'*

Cover Design By StreetWise Publications
ISBN 978-1-4716-4754-3

Published by StreetWise Publications
22 Waikanda Cres, Whalan, NSW 2770
http://thewordshop.info
http://streetwisepublications.info

Foreword

This is the fourth Rorschach anthology, a true montage indeed. We open with some poignant prose as Jerome L. Jones remembers his time in Vietnam with two works, '*Road Sweep*' and '*Mamma San*'. Jerry's work includes a eulogy to a fallen comrade and a moving poem. As a former soldier myself, I certainly empathise with the writer and the writing.

Our next Rorschach writer is Miriam Skerra. Miriam gives us the pleasure of some clever, out of the envelope pieces such as '*Narendra And The Butterfly*' and '*Short Story*' as well as some other pieces. Miriam's writing exhibits that unique blend of two languages many bilingual writers exhibit.

Vicki Barrington, on the other hand, is a native speaker and she has given us two solid short stories, perhaps even making it to novella status. '*The Whiz Kid Of Wall Street*' tells us of greed gone a little awry and '*Julia's Story*' has a suspenseful twist that dares the reader to keep turning the pages until the climax.

We also have Marianne Conlon's moving story of '*Pete And Mary*'. It reads like a true story, perhaps because for too many of us it is true. But spare a thought for the Pete's who have no Mary.

Our final contributor, no doubt used to being listed last alphabetically, is Jorge Zeledon. Jorge also writes in an adopted language, telling his very moving and intimately personal story of courage and hope in '*Hola Zorro!*' Jorge escaped war torn Nicaragua and knows first hand the desperation of the displaced.

Enjoy this, the fourth Rorschach, '*The Rorschach Montage*' and if you, too wish to become a published writer, visit us at www.thewordshop.info and we will be happy to welcome you to the fold.

Perry Gamsby
Sydney, March 2012

Jerome L. Jones

Jerome L. Jones was born in Independence, Missouri, USA and served his country for four years as a US Marine, including a tour in Vietnam. His writing of those events spans the gap of nearly half a century yet the reader knows they are still very vivid and very much remembered in the mind of the author.

Jerry met his wife , Elaine, while on R&R in Sydney during his year in Vietnam. On his discharge from the service he returned to Australia and they were married, bringing up four children and still living together in Fairfield West, NSW.

ROAD SWEEP

It had been an eventful week in his life to say the least. He had been 'in country' for seven days, and being the latest FNG, he had managed to be made to feel right at home by the old salts of the radio relay platoon These were hardened, cynical men who had been incountry longer than they cared to remember. Their average age was no more than twenty years. Everyone here counted the days until they could go back, back to the world and perhaps one day forget the experience of ever being in Vietnam. The countdown started the day you arrived and ended the day your Boeing 707 roared down the runway at Da Nang air base. Yeah, in country for seven days and he had already seen his first dead enemy and been knocked senseless by a black marine who resembled Mohammed Ali in build. He had destroyed his brain with too many drugs, his name was Jackson and living proof Vietnam had a very bad effect on people.

Last night he had pulled guard duty for the first time and now, as the guard was assembled for inspection and roll call, he heard his name called as a member of that day's road sweep. This was a function of the previous night's guard roster. Two squads of nine marines each were formed to walk on either side of the road leading to Da Nang. Two engineers with mine detectors would lead in the middle of the road. The two squads of marines would follow them and a tank brought up the rear. The tank was a great comfort because the Viet Cong would not attack a tank.

The morning still had a chill in the air and he could see the mist lifting above the rice paddies that surrounded the base camp of the 7th Marine Regiment. It reminded him of the early morning trips he went on with his friends and sometimes, his dad. They would go rabbit hunting or just shooting down by the Missouri River. But his wasn't home and the job he was here to do could turn deadly in the blink of an eye. Still, he was struck by beauty of Vietnam as the sun warmed the air under a cloudless blue sky. His reverie was broken by the Sgt. of the Guard's bellowing command to 'saddle up'. Eighteen marines stood up straight and took up their positions in their respective squads. Flak jackets and cartridge belts were checked and helmets were placed on heads. Next came the command to 'lock and load' and eighteen M-16s were loaded with magazines and cocked almost simultaneously. The Sgt. of the Guard called 'Ah ten hut!' followed by 'For'ard Harch'! They all knew the drill and could stay in step in silence if required. This particular morning the Sgt. of the Guard decided to call cadence until the road sweep was outside the gates and on the road to Da Nang. Once they were outside the gates he ordered 'route march' to indicate they could walk at a comfortable pace and not keep in step. The road sweep would continue up the road toward Da Nang until they met the road sweep from 1st Battalion, 7th Marines coming from the opposite direction. They would cover a distance of about two miles.

As they walked along the road all eyes were watching the stands of cane, brush and rice paddies for any signs of an ambush, while the engineers in the middle of the road searched for the enemy's favorite weapon - the land mine. These deadly devices took many forms and, depending on their size, could kill or maim a man or even obliterate a tank with six inch thick armor. They were normally triggered either by a hand generator or the pressure of a foot or vehicle tire or tractor tread. Of course the job of the road sweep was to detect and destroy these devices before they could be used by the enemy.

As they approached a village half a click(kilometre) from the base, he was alert to any change in the attitude or movements of the villagers. His twenty odd pounds of equipment was already causing him to sweat and he could tell today's heat was going to be as oppressive as that of past days. The villagers were going about their business without any attention to him or the other marines as the road sweep made it's way toward Da Nang. The kids of the village stood silent and watched through dark eyes as the marines made their way to the far end of their village. One kid being more adventurous than the rest called to him as he passed "Hey Joe, you got a smoke"? He shook his head no. He hadn't been in country long enough to experience the boredom that caused too many to take up that habit. He felt conspicuous as he walked through the village. He had not been issued with jungle greens yet. It had something to do with longshoremen back in the world sympathizing with the communist cause. He couldn't understand how anyone who lived in the greatest democracy in the world and enjoyed the freedoms afforded by that country would ever want to have a communist system of government. Coming from the Midwest, the Heart of America, he had been raised on the American version of history, the Good Book and Mom's apple pie. He had been taught 'the American Way' in school. He truly believed in it the same as he believed in God, Jesus Christ, and the Ten Commandments. At the age of twenty, there were no shades of gray.

The road sweep left the village behind and he focused his attention on the stands of bamboo, tall grass and rice paddies. There were also clumps of trees that shaded the occasional farmhouse standing like an oasis amidst the rice paddies. Seeing a farmer out in the field walking behind a water buffalo pulling a plough it was hard to believe a war was raging all around such a tranquil scene. The distant sound of artillery fire and the constant coming and going of helicopters and jet fighters made the scene surreal.

The marines were a full click past the village when his life suddenly changed. He was passing a large field of tall grass on his left. On the other side of the road, there was grassy flat land. This was studded with small trees twisted into tortured shapes by the wind and flood waters from the river that wound its way past the 7th Marines base camp. The sound of the bullet that went past his head was unmistakable. He had heard that sound many times before during live firing when he was in training. The loud crack and buzzing sound as it passed his head from the left told him it had come very close, too close. Someone shouted 'Sniper'! "Take cover'! The marines ran toward the river side of the road and jumped into the ditch below the road. The patrol commander barked "Anyone hit"? "No, Sir" came the reply from all of the marines. All eyes were searching the other side of the road to see if they could spot the sniper. He saw that he was directly opposite the large field of tall grass that had been on his left His mouth was suddenly dry and his heart was pounding as though he had just run a hundred yards. He had never been fired on before and it was not an experience he would like to have repeated.

He hadn't noticed before, but there was a narrow path running through the middle of the field. As he looked at the path, there was movement in the field to the left of the path. He couldn’t' t see anything. The grass was six feet tall. His heart was still pounding like it would soon leap out of his chest. He brought his rifle up just as the blur of a figure burst out of the grass and started running up the path away from the marines on the side of the road. Was this the one who just tried to kill me, he thought? The saliva in his mouth had dried up as he tried to see through the grass. He knew the runner in the field was as good as dead. The distance between them was a little less than fifty feet; point blank range for a marine rifleman. As the adrenalin rushed through his veins, he struggled to get control of his emotions. He remembered the weapons training he had at the rifle range. "Take up the slack slowly and evenly. Don't anticipate the recoil. Focus on the target. Breathe easy, squeeze the trigger, slow and even pressure". Now he was in no hurry as followed the running figure through the sight of his rifle, allowing for the increasing distance as his target moved away from him. It was textbook to him. This was what he had been trained to do. He had a picture in his mind of what was to happen when he put the last quarter ounce of pressure on the trigger. He would feel a slight bump as the M-16 in his shoulder sent it's lethal projectile toward his quarry. He imagined the shock the running figure would feel and the look of surprise on his face when his chest exploded and the force of the impact pitched him headlong into the dirt. His faceless enemy would literally be dead without knowing what hit him. He was still following the runner in his sights taking his time. Sweat formed above his brow as he struggled to control his breathing. His mouth was incredibly dry and his pulse echoed in his ears. Just a little more pressure on the trigger and it would be over. He will have made his first kill - a human being. It would be one less Viet Cong. His quarry was fast disappearing up the path through a sea of grass. He had to fire now or take a chance on missing the faceless runner. It was then he saw her. She was in his sights, standing near the end of the path, waving franticly and calling to the running figure. He saw behind her the house where she and her son lived. He released his pressure on the M-16's trigger. "OK, on your feet" called the patrol commander. "The sweep from 1st Battalion will be waiting for us up ahead". Seventeen marines scrambled back onto the road brushing dust from their uniforms, cursing the unseen enemy. One marine climbed up the roadway and, as he stood up, wiped the sweat from his face with a shaking hand. There would be many more days like this one. For the first time, he realized he was not invincible. Today, he had just been lucky.

CHARLIE

Charlie Prevedel was a good kid as a boy. Fairly quiet but not in an introverted way. He was adopted by Sarah and Frank who could not have children naturally. As parents they were great for Charlie. Being a former catholic nun, Sarah was strict but she loved the boy dearly as did Frank. Charlie was soon joined by another adopted child; this time it was a girl, Judith. A few years after Judy came into their lives, Sarah fell pregnant. It was a real surprise especially to Sarah and Frank who thought they would never conceive a child. Joseph Prevedel duly arrived at his appointed time and Charlie and Judith finally had a brother.

We would spend a weekend visiting Sarah and Frank where they lived in St. Louis a couple of times a year. Frank and Sarah were very down to earth people and made everyone feel right at home. Frank had a very dry sense of humor. He had been in the navy in World War II and while in the navy he got appointed the ships' barber. He continued his career as a barber after the war on a strictly casual basis. Frank had even installed a real hydraulic barber's chair in the basement. As soon as we entered the house, Frank would remark to Dad that I looked pretty shaggy and needed my ears lowered. That was the signal for Frank, Dad and me to adjourn to Frank's barber shop for a couple hours of torturing me. The two men would smoke cigars and chat while Frank would take a snip at my hair every once in a while. Frank and Dad would eventually release me and I would spend the rest of the weekend running wild with Charlie and the rest of the kids.

Charlie was also a talented musician. He played the piano accordion, the organ and the electric guitar. Charlie was asked to play at every family gathering and he would amaze everyone with his talent especially when he played the accordion. He inspired me to learn to play the accordion but I could never play as good as Charlie could.

Charlie was a few years older than me so we didn't have too much in common when I was younger. When he started high school, I still had a few years of primary school left. Charlie was a real outdoors man. He liked to go hunting and he had a hunting dog, a beagle, who would flush out rabbits for Charlie who never missed. He would sometimes take me out with him and he talked about joining the army and would tell me all about the latest martial arts moves he had learned. Charlie eventually joined the army. Sarah and Frank didn't think the army would take him because Charlie had a rare eye condition that required a special prescription. Uncle Sam wasn't very particular at the time so Charlie was duly enlisted and he loved life in the army. He did two tours in South Korea and then qualified as a Green Beret.

By the time Charlie went to Vietnam, I had finished my training in the marines and had received orders for Vietnam. I arrived in country 28 November 1968. I was stationed with 7th Marine Regiment. Because Charlie was with the Green Berets, I never knew exactly where he was in Nam. We had not corresponded over the years. I was shocked when I received the letter telling me Charlie was missing in action, presumed killed. The whole family hoped Charlie and his patrol would one day be found in some POW camp but as the years went by even that hope faded. In June 2004 my brother, Larry, called. The first thing he said was "They found Charlie". Larry then told me what facts had been given the family. Judy even had the battle report written by the NVA commander of the force that surrounded and overran Charlie's patrol. Charlie had been missing for thirty six years. The army had to identify Charlie from his special prescription glasses. They had approached his birth family but they would not give a DNA sample. No matter, because as far as I am concerned, Charlie was, is and always will be a member of my family of whom we are all justly proud. I wrote to Judy and sent the following poem to her. I was honored that she included it in Charlie's funeral service.

HOMECOMING

Lift my bones gently.
I yearn for my home.
Long have I lay on bloody field,
Lost and alone.

Carry me solemnly.
I am longing for home.
To lie in her soil
With comrades I've known.

Lay me out tenderly.
I am going home.
My loved ones still weeping,
Sister and brother the watch keeping.

Lower me slowly.
Bugler! Sound Last Post lowly.
Guard! Fire the salute!
In shining helmets and gleaming boots.

Cover me softly,
I am where I belong.
Let me rest. Go in peace.
I am home. I am home.

MAMMA SAN

Morning had broken at 7th Marines. It was only zero eight-hundred hours and it was already eighty degrees Fahrenheit. The humidity must have been ninety percent. The 7th Marine Regiment's base was on Hill 55, about twenty miles south of Da Nang. The scenery around the Marine base consisted of rice paddies that from the air resembled a patchwork quilt of different shades of green. To the south was a river with trees along either bank shading it's path as it flowed lazily down to the sea. The mountains in the distance to the west were breathtaking in the mornings as the mist rose from the fields. Altogether a tranquil scene that belied the violence and death that were dealt out regularly by both the warring sides. The farmers have been in the fields for hours already. It is planting time and everyone is working to get this season's rice crop planted. Life is hard here. People age quickly and their faces grow old and wrinkled long before their time.

I am sitting on a bench outside sick bay waiting to be seen by a medic. I had a multiple vaccination yesterday that left me with a fever. I am hoping to get some aspirin to take my temperature down. From the village down near the river about a click to the south a small group is making its way up to the front gate of the 7th Marines base. Two men are carrying a litter, one at either end. There is a woman with a couple of kids accompanying the stretcher bearers. The small party arrives and I see there is an old woman lying on the litter. Her hair is gray and her face is lined and wrinkled from living the life of a peasant working in the rice paddies under the blazing sun. The men gently lowered the stretcher to the ground next to me. The old woman's face is an awful ashen color and her eyes are glazed with only the slightest glimmer of life in them. She is labouring to breathe and every intake of air is painful. Her breathing is so shallow the rise and fall of her chest is almost indiscernible. The front of the old woman's clothing is covered in blood. She has obviously been badly wounded.

The younger woman in the group approaches the door of the medic hut followed by her two young children. She knocks on the door and a medic opens the door.

"What do you want"? he asks irritably. "We don't treat civilians here".

The young Vietnamese woman asks for a doctor to look at her mother, Mamma San. She has great difficulty because she doesn't speak his language. The medic bombards her with questions as to how Mamma San came to be wounded, how old is she, when was she wounded? The daughter manages to answer the questions she understands using a combination of broken English and hand gestures.

"You people know we can't treat civilians here" the medic complained "take her to the hospital in Da Nang".

"But Sir," the young woman replied, "Mamma San hurt. Last night in village. Big explosion. Mamma San hurt bad. She needs doctor."

Suddenly, another man appears at the door. He is wearing a gold oak leaf on his collar indicating the rank of a commander in the US Navy. He is the medical officer in charge of the field hospital at 7th Marine Regiment.

"We can't treat civilians here. It is against policy." he says gruffly.

"Please help Mamma San" the young woman pleaded, "she needs doctor".

"I am a doctor", the commander replied, " and I am telling you we cannot treat her here!"

"But if she not help, she die!"

At that the doctor's attitude softened,

"How was Mamma San injured?"

"Last night in village, big explosion!" she said gesturing with her hands the intensity of the blast.

"Was Mamma San out setting boobytrap for Number one Marines?"

"No, She asleep in house and big explosion hurt her!" the daughter explained. The woman then told the commander in broken English that a 'short round' had landed in their village and destroyed the house occupied by Mamma San.

"Bring her inside" the doctor said.

The woman spoke to the two litter bearers in Vietnamese. They lift the stretcher and take Mamma San into sick bay. They exit immediately and take up positions outside, squatting in the fashion that is typical of the people here. I notice their skin their faces tanned dark by endless hours spent under a savage sun. Their hands were the calloused tough hands of farmers the nails black from working in the paddies.

By now the sun was baking everything in the camp. The doctor and medic started working on Mamma San in the sick bay. They questioned the old woman's daughter about her age, general health etc. She tried to answer but most of what they asked her she didn't understand. The doctor kept asking the young woman how Mamma San was injured and each time she gave the same explanation about a 'short round'. The medics scoffed at this explanation saying Mamma San must have been out setting boobytraps for Marines. No sympathetic M.A.S.H. medicos here. No Hawkeye Pierce sickened by the sight of mangled civilians at this field hospital.

The doctor was now using suction to clear Mamma San's wounds. After some minutes he decided it was futile and announced to Mamma San's daughter, "There's not much can be done for her here. She's got pneumonia and her lungs are filling with fluid. We could send her to the hospital in Da Nang but the outcome will still be the same. It would be better to take her home where she will be with people she knows when the end comes."

With that, the young woman came out of the sick bay carrying one child on her hip with the other clinging to her black silk pants. She put on the slightly conical straw hat of a peasant and spoke in Vietnamese to the two men waiting outside. The men, who had not uttered a word since arriving, got up and went inside. They reappeared carrying Mamma San on the litter to take her home one last time. There were no tears, in fact, no show of emotion at all. Just the silent stoicism I had seen many times before. They all left as they had arrived, in silence. The next afternoon there was a fresh grave in the village cemetery. Death is a large part of life here, no matter how it comes.

Miriam Skerra

Miriam Skerra is originally from Germany and says she writes and thinks in both languages, but not a the same time.

Miriam's clever prose, cheeky wit and fresh look at topics balances out the other writing in this anthology.

Miriam currently lives in Sydney, NSW

A SHORT STORY

"I am almost ready!" exclaimed Novel, the novel to be, waiting to be born.

"No, you're not! You haven't got a plot!" remarked the poem, calling out from its incubation chamber.

"Shut up!" retorted Novel, "You are not only undeveloped, you haven't even formed any details nor have you got a plan or purpose. All you do is rhyme! We all can do that! So get back to it and take on some form before you come out!"

"Me first, me first! Me first, oh how I thirst to come out first yet I am cursed. I may just burst to come out first!" Poem replied, hoping to make an impression, jumping up and down on his unstable little feet.

"You cannot be taken seriously!" Novel dismissed Poem "You just blurt out meaningless words. You have rhyme without reason! Stop being selfish! As for me, it has taken me years to collect material from our host. All you do is hold me up with your annoying penetrating noise! All I need now is putting everything I've collected together, all my bits and pieces. Oh where is my head(ing). I haven't got a foot to stand on yet!"

"Why don't you get yourself sorted out and let me come out first!" Short Story suggested. Novel pricked up his ears. This could buy him time for some more inspiration. While Short Story was coming out first Novel could develop, gain hand and foot, find his rhythm and take on shape. Turning his attention to Short Story he asked, "How long have you been around? I haven't even noticed you!"

"Hmmm, to be honest, I haven't developed at all. All I know is that I have been asked to come out."

"What? You have been asked to come out? Hahaha, that's funny! You haven't got an idea yet what and who you are, but you want to come out? Hahahaha!" laughed Novel.

"To be honest I don't feel like coming out. It's only that…." Short Story was not even able to finish his sentence for he felt frightened.

"What?" prodded Novel, "What do you mean?"

"Well…" Short Story timidly answered "I have been asked to be published!"

Novel grew very jealous in an instant and he blushed and puffed up like a liver after a bottle of Scotch. "You want to be published, do you?" he snuffed at Short Story in a fit of envy. His anger was short-lived though as he saw Short Story cringe in fear. "I am sorry, little story. I didn't mean it. Just tell me, who asked you to be published?"

"A guy named Perry…"

"Who? Do I know him? Who is he? Is he a guru?"

"Yes, he is a guru."

"Do you feel intimidated by him?"

"Yes!" Short Story sobbed. "I thought I was ready, I thought I was so clever and confident and ready to jump into the pen to be written. 'The pen is mightier than the sword' I thought. Just when I was about to pounce onto the paper, Perry said all these things to frighten me. Things like '10,000 words' and 'don't use the "t-word"'."

"What?" Novel was intrigued: "don't use a t-word?"

"Sssh! Hush! I am not to use the word 'the'"

"Oh I see! That is interesting. Ha, sorry Shorty, you have used 'the' already several times just then!"

"I won't tell Perry. Please don't tell Perry, will you?"

"I won't tell Perry anything just yet. Remember, I neither have hand nor foot!"

"So many restrictions!" Short Story sighed. "I don't think I can do it. Ten thousand words! I don't even know how much I have got to ramble to make it to that."

"The the the the the" Poem butted in, appearing from the background.

"You will be my ruin!" Short Story desperately remarked, trying hard to ignore Poem.

"Nothing rhymes with 'the'" Poem remarked. Poem, jumpy little critter, had nothing but mischief on his mind. To tease Short Story even more he continued, "The theophany of theologian Theodor resulted in the theoretic theorem of the thesis in the theatre of Thessalonica!"

Short Story was close to giving up when Novel silenced Poem with these commanding words, "True poems are not loud. True poems are poetic, even pathetic, lyrical, yes, not hysterical."

Poem felt embarrassed, realising that Novel had spoken wisely and meaningful, plus his words had also rhymed and made sense in their context.

Poem retreated for respite so as not to be repeated.

Novel and Short Story revelled in Poem's absence and began to consult on ways to capture ideas, have them written down so Short Story could be published.

"I am so full of ideas! I wish somebody could help me put them all together."

"I am glad you asked" a deep voice from beyond retorted.

"Who are you?" both Short Story and Novel called out in surprise.

"I am Essay" Essay said in a matter-of-fact way.

"I hadn't noticed you. Have you been in here for long?"

"You mean have I been in this host for long? Yes, I have been listening to all of you, your raised tempers, your jealous struggle, your misconceptions. You waste so much energy getting nowhere."

"Are you going to be published?" Short Story enquired, feeling a twinge of jealousy. Mixed with hope for relief from having to go out first.

"I will eventually come out. When it is my time. Right now I am here to tell you what your problem is, You need to settle! Relax! You all want to come out, be presented and become famous. I ask you, Does anyone go out without getting dressed, washing their face, brushing their teeth, combing their hair and having a good look in the mirror? No, not if they want to be presentable. You need to be more composed to start with! Why do you look so uncomfortable again, Short Story?"

"You used 'the'. You said 'the mirror'" Short Story answered as quietly as he could, hoping Perry wouldn't hear it.

"Oh how easily intimidated you are!" Essay felt like shouting. Instead, he spoke matter-of-factly in prose, "You are easily intimidated and distracted. Perry was simply asking you to experiment. He did not say you were not allowed to use 'the' ever, he simply gave you an idea how to direct and command your words by drawing your attention to formulation, substitution and variety of wordings.

"Oh" Short Story inclined his ear and became more introverted, looking at his wordings.

Essay continued, "Look at the instruction as help rather than as restriction. Look how haphazard, floaty and dispersed you have been. Perry's instructions will help you find a range. They will open new vistas and provide new tools for you to work with to find out more about yourself. You want to be published fully composed, directed, clear, concise and structured."

Novel countered, "With all due respect Sir, you sound boring. You are so prosey! What about creativity, crazy ideas, new invention, unorthodox composition, unconventional delivery? What's wrong with that?"

"Okay. That's what you are a novel for. You are allowed all that of course. You also, Short Story, are permitted to be all of that. No-one wants to restrict your creativity. I only want to help you to construct and build so as to be readable. That is if you want to be read by anyone? If you have got something to say you must find a way to sustain your story so the reader is compelled to read it to its end and feel himself/herself inspired. Ask yourself, what is your objective? So…what is your objective by the way?"

Short Story hesitated for a while, still lost in contemplation before he answered, "I used to know what I wanted. There is pressure to accomplish myself, to be ready to come out in ten thousand words. Yet I do not know how much that is. There is a time frame. I have to be out within 8 weeks. In fact I should have started to come out."

"Why don't you let the pen take care of that?" Novel suggested.

Essay wisely answered on Short Story's behalf: "He's got writer's block! This condition is often caused by pressure we think is from outside but have taken on and internalised. That's why I am taking my time with coming out. I make sure I am completed and ready before I let anyone know I even exist."

"Me too!" Novel added.

Essay continued, "Short Story, you have not accepted Perry's advice for what it is. Instead of embracing it as the help it is you have used it as excuse for not coming out."

"You are saying 'the' too much" Short Story winced desperately.

"You are diverting the conversation. You are crying 'too hard' and should find someone else to blame for your procrastination. By the way, when did I say 'the'? Did I say 'the'?"

"You said '*the* help' just then."

"What else could I have said?" Essay put this question to Short Story to stimulate him to think of alternatives.

"Maybe you could have simply said 'advice' instead of 'the advice'?

"Yes, you are right. I could have omitted 'the'. It would not have carried the same meaning though. When I said 'you were not embracing Perry's advice for the help it is' the word 'help' was given a special weight and importance as a word by calling it '*the* help it is'. For example, you are Short Story. How would it feel, if you were *the* Short Story, *the one* people want to read, *the famous Short Story*. That would elevate you above simply being a short story, unread or read and then forgotten.

Maybe Perry's idea was for you to think about just that. Had he not asked you to not use 'the' this conversation would have never taken place."

"What if tomorrow he asks you to not use 'to', 'is' or 'and'? Then you'll be stuffed. Hahahaha" Novel teased.

"If I use words like 'the' a lot I can quickly get to ten thousand words as well. Perry said he wants ten thousand words for each short story."

Novel interrupted, "If you stopped worrying about coming up to ten thousand words you could feel free to use words so expressive and so full of meaning that Perry would be so absorbed in the story he would not even notice how short or long you are. Size does not matter! It is not about what you have got it's what you do with it! It is not about the words you use or don't use, it's about how they work and radiate, how they keep the reader intrigued, stimulated, involved, opening a world to them they have never seen, beckoning them to come along on a mind journey they have never travelled before, awakening senses they only know from dreams."

There was silence after that delivery. Both Essay and Short Story sat up and took notice as Novel spoke. Never had they heard such a speech. Even Poem, while staying low key in his retreat, pricked his ears and absorbed the words, feeling a vibration of inspiration, an inclination toward transpiration toward publication. He stopped himself in time to realise that he needed time and contemplation to mature and grow and become."

"How do we get our host to put us to paper?" Short Story asked, still feeling rushed. "Does she appreciate us for who we are? Will she know how to separate us and refine us? Has she got any skills at all? Are we trapped in here forever?"

"Hopefully she will consult with Guru Perry to learn how to lead us out, one by one."

"It is more important for me. Guru wants me to come out first" Short Story signalled.

"Are you so hung up on your stage fright?" enquired Novel.

"Is that what it is you think? I feel so worthless, I don't know why. I think I lost the plot. Oh, now I said 'the' again as well. How can anything ever become of me?"

"Don't worry, little Story, don't worry, you don't have to be perfect. You are only just little, like a child. You are the first one to come out – no-one expects any miracles from you." Novel comforted Short Story, trying to expel any panic he still felt.

"If you don't come to fruition it'll be our host's fault for not letting you out." Essay logically added. "I believe she is trying too hard to formulate us. She doesn't realise we are only words away from her success as writer. She may be more scared than you are! "

"Ha! Humans like to believe they created us. They always want all credit for themselves. If we ever get published who gets the credit? Our host does!" said Novel. "We are ideas who came from way out there, vibrations that entered a soul to take form in body. Yet people want to believe we are their invention.

Short Story cottoned on, "Do you think we can convince our host to be humble and accept that we are a gift she has the privilege of giving?"

"Oh, look at you! You are turning into a philosopher now, little Story!"

Essay, picking up the thought, continued, "Sometimes you find people who recognise that they are but instruments by saying what they are saying, by playing what they are playing. As they were saying, 'Nothing you can do that can't be done, nothing you can sing that can't be sung, nothing you can say but you can learn how to play the game. It's easy. Nothing you can make that can't be made, no-one you can save that can't be saved, nothing you can do but you can learn how to be you in time. It's easy. Nothing you can know that isn't known, nothing you can see that isn't shown, nowhere you can be that isn't where you're meant to be. It's easy. All you need is love all you need is love all you need is love, love, love is all you need.' I would like to acknowledge that this is a quote from a song that was written by John Lennon. He was someone who realised that his songs were a gift given to him to re-give. The words he penned and the music he produced were already there. He was the instrument who formulated them, who played 'the game' as he calls it."

"Hang on!" Short Story had a question, "You quoted a 'John Lennon'. Isn't that plagiarism?"

"No" stated Essay, "plagiarism is when you act like *you* created the words when in fact it was someone else who had said them before. Plagiarism is theft; stealing someone else's words"

"Oh, so I can actually quote others and might divert the limelight that way. I'll get the reader so focussed on the subject that they won't even notice me."

"Very good, Shorty! Nature itself is unselfconscious and to be natural is to be unselfconscious. Give credit to others and you will shine. Be unselfish, unassuming, unpretentious!"

"Hey Poem, have you got a final comment before we send Short Story out into the world?"

Will the reader feel inspired
As much as you were when you dreamt it?
Or will the reader just grow tired
Not understanding how you meant it?

Will the reader get the sense
Of why the story's written?
Will you gain many friends?
In the book, how will you fit in?

Never mind, you're just a first
Of many works to come
Even if you are the worst
At least you were having fun.

And if you lost the plot
Guru will get you fit.
On your way you learnt a lot
The journey sure was worth it

Out of the labyrinth of mind
Come pathos or come glory
Who knows what the reader may find
Come on! Complete the story!

Out is the story led
With help from the leader
The writer is dead.
Long live the reader!

"You have got a few weeks, Short Story. I suggest you go for a little beauty sleep. You'll feel better when you wake up. You will feel inspired by what you hear from the other writers' stories in our host's class. Off you go, Shorty, off you go!"

Exhausted, Short Story nodded off and dreamt…himself. And while he dreamt himself, his host picked up the pen and wrote…

NARENDRA AND THE BUTTERFLY

"I feel sorry for you! " Narendra the mathematician compassionately remarked while sitting in a beautiful bush land reserve, making his estimations. He was addressing a passing butterfly.

"Hmmhmmhmmh?" enquired Butterfly, flittering a little more haphazardly than usual before settling on the inflorescence of a *Buddleia.*

"I feel sorry for you because you have got only one month to live!" Narendra explained.

"Isn´t that the normal life-span?" asked Butterfly.

"Oh no! 80 to 90 years is a normal life span!"

Narendra shuddered at his own words as he realised that he had revealed the shocking truth regarding the life-span of butterflies.

"I make it up in wing-span, do I not?" Butterfly timidly and apologetically replied, as if a long life-span was a virtue. Humans obviously believed in a long life-span and Butterfly didn´t want to offend.

In an effort to diffuse the situation, in case he had hurt Butterfly's feelings, Narendra quickly responded:

"Yes, dear little Butterfly. Your wingspan is enormous compared to mine. Besides, you look very beautiful!"

This compliment humbled Narendra, as the recognition of another always does.

"Oh my God! " Narendra suddenly burst out, "My wing-span ought to be 2 meters and eighty if I was to be like you! You certainly are better equipped than me!"

"My wings are fragile and my life is short?" apologised the butterfly.

"So tell me, little butterfly… well, you´ve got a very large wing-span, you little beautiful one, but why on earth do you not fly straight? Have you not got your bearings right? Your wings are symmetric, but your flight certainly is not!"

"Hmmhmmhmmh? 'Why on earth?' you ask? Not on earth, in ether is my world! In multi-faceted air I live, smelling flowers, drinking nectar. Every second of my life I find another pretty niche. Why do humans walk past them, Narendra?"

Narendra, bewildered and intrigued by the question, gazed at the beauty of the butterfly's super-dimensional flight and realised that life itself was more than just a span measured in years. Just as the wing-span of a butterfly is in no direct relation to the distance travelled, so depth and beauty of life cannot be measured by a time-span.

Narendra´s mathematical mind took a sharp turn, a lateral side-step; almost like the flight-path of a butterfly ... fleeting, floating in fluid motion towards some of the infinite inner dimensions mathematics allows for, yet never delves into.

"You spend your 80, 90 years walking in one direction yet never arrive. What are your 80 years for? In my one month of life I am always there and I live, live and live, flying out the niches, the cosy little corners of life. I don´t have to go anywhere because I am already there. I am what your life will be when it is fulfilled."

"Oh what beautiful life! Exquisite and pure! A butterfly has taught me more about life in two minutes than 13 semesters at university did" Narendra humbly acknowledged.

Butterfly who felt equally grateful for the encounter with Narendra, smiled "Thank you for teaching me all these things!"

Then he flew off, stopped by a pink beautiful *Stylidium formosum*, took a sip and drunkenly staggered to the next flower.

FLOWERPOWER

Once upon a time three plants met in a garden; a melon, a cabbage and a flower. They loved each other so much they fused into a meloncauliflower. That´s why flowers inspire melancholy with people in love.

PERSONALITY AND CHARACTER

A personality and a character met on the street.
"You´ve got personality!" said the personality.
"Oh, thank you! You´ve got character" said the character.
That´s how we see ourselves in the other.

The little boy asked his Dad "What is a personality?"
"A person who has character"
"And what is a character?"
"A person who has personality"

IN THE JAPANESE GARDEN AT THE CAMPBELLTOWN ART GALLERY ON FRIDAY 11.02.2011

Lampions and childhood memories are hanging off the arches along the art gallery, fire-red and creamy white. The breeze sways them and if I was small like a beetle I would sit on one and have the ride of my life. The breeze gently blows my hair and if I was a louse I´d sit in it and have the ride of my life. But as it is, I am sitting in a Japanese teahouse, having the ride of my life in my imagination.

I use the tea house as my very personal room of contemplation and here I am the louse, the beetle, the me who is making the most of the features surrounding me. The cascade´s calming sound overrides the distant traffic. The silence in this garden expands soothingly into outer and inner space. My space is taken by this transcending contemplative stillness. No matter from which angle I look onto, into or out from the teahouse I see harmonious superior order, better than perfection. The diagonals of the structure glide into the garden which is contained by formations of trees, perfectly placed rocks and well-kept borders. Raked pebble grounds demand my respect, holding me at bay lest I tread on them and yet I feel endlessly free within this confinement. If you are not content you have declared yourself not to be part of this garden. Any discomfort from the heat is transformed into pleasure by the gentle fanning of the elm and cherry trees. Even the visuals, the pool, into which the brook cascades, the colours of the stone and simple wooden structure, cool my senses. The doorways and windows of the teahouse frame and draw attention to an infinite work of art by One who never shows, yet is always present. Everything around me is a monument of praise. Praise for whom or what? Do I need to know? This architecture, this garden and the innermost chamber of one's inner self seems to have become one.

Soon I will leave this spot, but something will go with me from here. Not anything tangible, not anything explicable, not anything fathomable; yet I will treasure it forever, even though it was but an hour only in my life. The hour expands into something within me, unending. Yet it was nothing but an hour of stillness in a garden. No notable love affair or great invention, not anything the world has never seen. Just an hour of being.

And it´s all I want. Ever.

Forever.

And ever.

INTERCITY EXPRESS

Being well acquainted with my kitchen, I notice when something is different. One day I spotted a moving thin streak or line, a train of tiny creatures moving through the enormous landscape of my domain. They all went the same path on the way to a curious destination on my bench top, others were on their way back from whatever mission they had been on. Sometimes the train seemed broken but quickly new creatures would follow the exact same trail. With my eyes I followed the caravan route which led to the curious destination. What's an intercity express doing in my kitchen? I thought. I looked closer at the individual carriages and noticed they all had their own engine. Six tiny hairlike legs propelled them in a most steady rolling rhythm toward their goal. At some places the train seemed broken; where the first carriage of the oncoming traffic would meet there was a little break in movement as the two conductors seemed to exchange some information which appeared intricately complex. I couldn´t quite make out whether they were sniffing each other like dogs or whether they talked *AntLan*, a silent language they would have mastered from their infancy. It must have been some type of shorthand as it takes me lots longer to explain directions when someone asks *me* and even longer to *understand* directions when someone explains them to me. Well, some people just look at each other and understand (and I was certainly not ever blessed with such a gift), but that a whole tribe, a whole nation should travel through Titan's territory in an unfamiliar giant landscape, a land so vast...

As my eyes followed them in the direction of their destination I beheld that they had struck gold! Here was the essence of history relived. People used to come from all directions to the Wild West in search for gold and feared no enemy. Here in the territory I was the master of ants were crowding around a golden lake, filling their invisible backpacks with the speck of honey they had undertaken their incredible journey for. I guess they had backpacks or some sort of storage compartments, too tiny to see. I was struck with wonder as I began to realise that these tiny folk, finders of honey, were just as destined to conquer and clean out my kitchen as I must surely be, playing a part in being watched by grander beings as I rummage through their territory in a world on a planet that we think belongs to us.

Thinking myself so much more powerful than an ant I puffed up my chest and said 'Hey you little pipsqueaks, what do you think you are doing?'

Having different ideas about my kitchen than these tiny people I decided to employ a trick. I removed the spot of honey, carefully shooing the gathering of slurping munchkins and broke their track somewhere halfway between their gold mine and the exit, where house meets garden and where they marched freely under the door as if under a gigantic bridge. I used my finger to rub hard across their path. After some initial disturbance they quickly gathered their wits even though their communication time was enormously lengthened from one to two and a half seconds and their sign language became lots more complex. Behold where the track was broken the incoming train stopped and most ants returned as they seemed to have been informed that the jackpot had been taken.

As I am a busy house-wife I now gave attention to making beds, cleaning windows, washing clothes. When I returned to look at the longest ICE I had ever encountered, it was gone.

My kitchen was clean and cleared of invaders. Thank goodness there were no casualties at the derailment, which I´m proud to announce.

I marvel at you, little geniuses! Who governs you, tiny folk?

A tiny incident with tiny participants has given me a tiny idea of something infinitely grand. Am I a link in a train, on a track of an invisible path?

Vicki Barrington

I dedicate these stories to my family; without them life would be boring.

Vicki Barrington is a wife, mother and grandmother. She has been writing short stories for a number of years.

She gets inspiration from her friends and family and enjoys writing fictional stories that captivate and involve the reading audience, by trying to create a visual scene in the reader's mind.

Vicki likes to write because it opens up the unending realm of possibilities that fiction gives, Enjoyment and to please the reader is her aim, and she hopes that her work will do just that.

THE WHIZ KID OF WALL STREET

Chapter One

Jamie lay on the bed, hands resting on his chest as he watched the smoke from his cigarette rise up to the peeling paint on the ceiling. He rose from the old metal bed, the springs creaked loudly from age and decay. He crushed out the cigarette in the overfilled ashtray.

The dirty dishes from the previous night sat unwashed in the discoloured sink. The discarded food scraps and containers, were a nightly feast for the family of cockroaches that crawled out from behind the cracked and stained wall. " His little buddies", he called them. Although he hated creepy crawlies, he had grown quiet fond of them in a way.

The darkened room was illuminated by the full moon coming through the grimy window of this one room apartment. He sat at the table and looked at the pile of newspapers he had collected. His eyes moved to the black duffle bag, he opened it and looked in. Four million dollars stared back at him. He sat back and laughed to himself.

The Whiz Kids of Wall Street they called me…he thought to himself.

"Yeah and what a Whiz I was." he said out loud, smiling with deep satisfaction. Just think it couldn't have been possible without you, my old pal Lenny. He leaned back on the odd stained wooden chair, nothing matched in this place. Jamie started to think back to how it all began.

Chapter Two

Jamie Blake, twenty-six years old, intelligent, quick witted, college honour graduate, mathematical whiz. He had joined the stockbroking firm of Lane, Taylor and Hampton as a junior floor runner, but his expertise on the market and knack for buying and selling of stocks at the right time, soon earned him a superior reputation and a promotion along with a raise. His phone constantly rang from companies and investors that wanting him to take their money and invest. He made millions for multi million dollar companies. The one thing they all had in common, were the more he made them the more they wanted. And most of all none were willing to share their good fortune with anyone. Especially with the one that made it for them.

One evening Jamie sat in his office, waiting on a call from one of the partners. He and Justin Hampton were both up for a promotion, although Justin was Hampton's nephew, Jamie knew the promotion would be his, as he had been there nineteen months longer and had built up a hefty clientele for the company, plus his reputation and judgment were impeccable.

He thought of packing up his belongings, as the promotion would mean a move up to the 37th floor and maybe his own office instead of a corner workstation.

The phone finally rang,

"Jamie, William Taylor here, still working I see." he said

"Just finishing up a few loose ends Sir," thankful Taylor couldn't see the game of solitaire on his computer.

"Just a quick call Jamie," he hesitated, "We...errr...have given the promotion to Justin… but that is not to say, we don't value your commitment to the company and your drive to do well. So don't be disheartened, there are more promotions on the horizon and you are well and truly up there with the others…so..err.. I will have to run, meetings you know how it is, see you tomorrow, bye" Taylor rung off.

Jamie sat there for a long time, the phone dangling from his fingers….how could they do this to him…Justin didn't know half as much as he did. It was a case of who you know, not what you know.

He was seething. He turned off his computer and went home.

Chapter Three

Lenny Collis was a young man, with his life ahead of him. He was friendly, easy going and strong, He had worked for his uncle in the construction business; his uncle Mike had high hopes for this hard working young man. But then, in the blink of an eye it was all taken away from him. The car accident had claimed both parents instantly. Lenny was hospitalised for almost 5 months. His leg would never heal, he would walk with a permanent limp. Lenny had also suffered slight brain damage, which affected his speech and memory. The hospital bills where piling up and Lenny had no choice but to sell his parents house to pay for the bills and his parents funerals.

While he recovered, Lenny was assigned a welfare case worker, named Miles Harries. He was fond of Lenny and helped him find a place to live, when he finally left the hospital. It was in an older walk up apartment on the 3rd floor of a tenement down near the docks.

But Lenny didn't mind, in fact, he loved it, he called it The Penthouse, as it was the only apartment with roof top access. Miles had managed to get a few bits and pieces of furniture from his parent's house before the sale, so he would be able to have something familiar around him. Lenny had asked him to get the two deck chairs, he had built with his father, for his mother and he loved them, they reminded him of his parents. He set them out on the roof under an old beach umbrella. Miles had put some potted plants around the small roof top area and it looked just like his own little garden and Lenny was happy; alone, but happy.

Lenny's life was the same routine, each morning he would go to the corner and buy the paper from Joe the paper guy on the corner. He would then go to the diner around the corner and have coffee and a bagel with cream cheese, his favourite. Stella, the waitress, always served Lenny and would always greet him with.

“Hi there handsome, usual today?” she would ask with a smile.

Lenny always replied. “Y-y-yes please” and returned her smile.

Stella liked Lenny, she felt sorry for this kid who always sat alone in the corner booth, reading the paper while eating his bagel. Each morning he would read first, the funny pages and then he would look up the Daily Shipping News. It was Lenny’s dream to one day get a job as a deckhand on one of the big tankers or container ships. He would work his way around the world and see the sites and cultures of other countries, he and his mother used to talk about when he was growing up.

Sometimes in the shipping news, companies would advertise for deckhands. Lenny would always watch for these positions, but he knew that he had to get ‘a bit better first’, before he could apply. Often Lenny would go down to the docks and watch the ships unload the containers onto the waiting semi-trailers, or watch the cranes stack them on the docks. He would stay there until sunset, and then make his way back to The Penthouse, before it got too late. Being out on the streets in this neighbourhood at night could be dangerous.

Chapter Four

One evening working late as he often did Jamie started to invent a game on his computer. He had an idea of moving some of his client's money around from different accounts to a fictitious company, then to see if he could trace it. It couldn't be traced if he buried it deep enough.

What started out as a game on his computer, became a deadly game of greed and deceit. But it was just a game. Until... Until Jamie was once again passed over for promotion, after more "family members" joined the company. There was the usual excuse and promises but he had had enough of them.

"This time I won't get mad," he said "I'll get even."

The computer game with other people's money suddenly got serious. He decided to call his company Whiz Kid Inc. There was almost $4 million in this account, and no one seemed to be any the wiser. Only he knew the account number, and down in the vault sat his $4 million. It could only be accessible for a short time, so he needed a plan before the money was missed. Once a month, quiet substantial sums of money was deposited into the vault in his building. It was for " tax purposes". Many companies would deal in cash only. So he knew he had to devise a plan that would coincide with this delivery.

He turned off his computer just as his cell phone rang.

"Jamie, it's Isaac, just letting you know your car is finished, you can pick it up anytime"

"Thanks Isaac, what's the damage? And what time do you close shop?"

"We are here till six, but I can wait if you like, oh and its $158"

Jamie knew if he left now he could make it before six. "Ok, thanks, see you soon"

He hurried down to the street, just as the #7 downtown bus pulled up outside his office building. He jumped on instead of rushing down almost five and a half blocks. There was a spare seat next to a dishevelled young man, but he didn't care it was a place to sit.

"H-h-hello J-j-jamie" the young man said quietly next to him.

Startled Jamie turned and looked at the man seated beside him. Suddenly he recognized the young man.

"Lenny..?? Is that you man? God its good to see you!" said Jamie shaking Lenny's hand. Jamie suddenly remembered what a friend had told him about Lenny's accident.

"Sorry to hear about your folks Lenny, they were really good people, your mom, she was a real special lady, and your dad was a good guy".

Lenny just nodded and thanked him for his kind words.

"What are you doing with yourself these days?" said Jamie.

"Not m-m-much, can't work n-n-no more, on wel-f-fare." Lenny stammered.

Jamie felt sorry for Lenny they had been such good friends in college. Looking up Jamie realized his stop was almost there.

"Look, tell you what, give me your address and I'll come by and we can have a couple of beers and pizza, talk about old times, would you like that?"

Jamie took out his pocket palm card and put in Lenny's address. He stood up and pushed the button for the next stop.

"I'll come and see you, how about Friday night, that ok with you?"

"Sure i-s-s," replied Lenny.

"See you then," Jamie jumped off the bus, and left Lenny smiling.

Chapter Five

Jamie sat on his apartment terrace drinking a beer, the lazy hot nights were coming to an end as summer faded and fall began. He popped the lid off another beer, thinking back to when he and Lenny had shared a dorm room college. They looked so much alike that people often mistook them for twins; they both had blonde messy hair, blue eyes and were even the same height and build. They would sit across the room from each other in class and confuse the teachers. Just when the teacher sorted out who was who, at the break they would change places, just to start the confusion all over again. They even had some girls convinced that they were twins separated at birth, but by some strange twist of fate, they met up at college,

"How bizarre " they would say.

The stupid thing was, they actually believed it!

He remembered the sad day when Lenny's mom had called to say his dad had been rushed to hospital with a heart attack. The doctors' said he couldn't work again. It was terrible for poor Lenny, when he finally returned to college, he made the decision to leave, to go and work construction for his Uncle Mike. He said if his dad couldn't work then it was up to him to help out his family. It was a difficult decision, but he had no choice. They thought it was only fitting that they play one last prank on someone they both detested.

"Sandy McAllister." they both chimed together.

Sandy McAllister was the head of the cheerleaders. She looked down her nose at

everyone. She was blonde, beautiful, had a killer body and she knew it! She would walk around with her little entourage bowing and scraping after her, like she was some kind of princess or something. Jamie had asked her out one time and she had embarrassed him in front of everyone.

Her answer was, "Please, you are a no body, run away little man, you are bothering me" she said.

Jamie stood there humiliated and embarrassed, as they all laughed at him.

Lenny remembered hearing her talk about some guy; she said he was as slimy as a snake.

"Those slimy disgusting animals, the only good snake is a dead snake." she spat with as much venom.

So off they went to the novelty store and purchased a life like rubber snake. They sneaked around the back of the girls' dorm and waited till they all went to cheerleading practice. Quietly they made their way up to Sandy's room, they all knew her room, if faced the gardens of the dorm. Jamie placed the snake under her pillow on her baby doll monogrammed pyjamas.

They sat on a bench opposite the dorm and waited. The girls came back just as it was getting dark. The light came on in her room; it was about fifteen minutes later long enough for her to shower, when they heard the blood curdling scream! Followed by another lot of screams from other girls.

They ran behind the bushes and rolled around laughing as the screams continued.

Chapter Six

Jamie was actually looking forward to seeing Lenny on Friday night. He knew the area was down near the docks and it wasn't a very pleasant neighbourhood, it was more like a ghetto and pretty rough. Jamie wore old clothes as not to draw attention to himself, especially in this part of the city.

Lenny's eyes lit up when he answered the door and saw Jamie standing there with a pizza and a six-pack.

"Y-y-you c-came" said Lenny smiling broadly.

"Sure did, said I would didn't I."

They talked and talked and Jamie started to get the story of Lenny's dismal life, since the accident. The ghetto in which he lived, the isolation having no friends or family a round him. Jamie was close to tears at times.

They agreed Jamie would pick him up the next Friday night and take him out for dinner and true to his word he picked Lenny up and took him out to a place Lenny had never been to, they ate dinner and talked about old times, Lenny had difficulty remembering some of the things they spoke about, but he would laugh along with Jamie anyway.

They enjoyed each others company and Jamie was happy that he and Lenny had met up again. Jamie would visit Lenny almost every Friday night, they would either go out to some place different each time or sometimes they would stay at Lenny's apartment with pizza and beers.

They spoke about old times and Jamie asked Lenny about his Uncle Mike. Mike used to give Lenny and Jamie worked on his construction sites so they could make some extra money for the summer.

Mike was the site manager and he always treated them well, the money was great, but they worked hard. It was back breaking work; they started at five-thirty sharp every morning. Lenny told him that his Uncle Mike was building a forty story office building about four blocks away, so they decided to go up there and check it out the next time Jamie came to visit.

Chapter Seven

Roderick Lawson and William Taylor, were standing behind Jamie in the canteen line at the company's cafeteria. They were discussing plans for the weekend and their usual Sunday morning golf game. Lawson said his in-laws were flying in for about 10 days, and he was to pick them up at the airport on Friday night. He said the flight got in about eight that night, so he would be able to make their four thirty afternoon meeting with the other partners.

Jamie listened intently as the money delivery would be coming in that Thursday evening. Jamie made sure he sat near Jane, Lawson's secretary, to hear any plans she may have for that week.

"The Rottweiler"…they called her, she made sure no-one got within ten feet of Lawson, unless she approved their appointments personally. He had to find out if she would be around at the time of the partner's meeting.

"Oh Lucy, you should see him," she gushed.

"He is just a dream and to think I didn't even want to go to that dinner party." Lucy sat, hanging on her every word, just eating, not speaking or even blinking. Apparently Jane had met the man of her dreams and she never stopped talking about him the whole lunch break. Jamie wondered if poor Lucy's ears were bleeding.

"Anyway he is picking me up at seven-thirty on Friday night, I can't wait. Oh and I managed with a lot of pleading and begging, to get an appointment with my Hairdresser, Mr. Rolo at five-thirty, so at five I'm outta here!"

Jamie listened smiling to himself. He had been waiting for this opportunity. Now to put Plan A into action. Hope it works, he thought as he didn't have a plan B. "Thanks Jane, you little darling, just what I have waited for" said Jamie to himself.

She had to be out by five, as her appointment with Mr Rolo was almost impossible to get, but she had managed to beg her way in with Robyn the owner of the salon. Jane wanted to look fantastic when Mr. Wonderful came to pick her up for their date. She had borrowed a little red number from her friend, after all what are friends for if you can't borrow their clothes, shoes, bags, hats.

Jane had tried on the dress she borrowed with the red pumps she bought to match the dress. Even she herself had to agree how great she looked but with a new hair style, she would be an absolute knockout!

Chapter Eight

Jamie sat at his workstation, it was eight minutes to five as he walked to the elevator and took it up to the thirty-seventh floor and rushed up to Jane's desk.

"Jane, thank god you're here" he said, breathing heavy as if he had run up the stairs from the ninth floor.

"What is it Jamie," demanded Jane, irritated.

"I have to get some files from Mr. Lawson's desk, he said that I would find them in his office, I have to deliver them to him tonight or my life is over!"

"What, he said nothing to me about that. God dam you Jamie, I have to be out of here in 2 minutes!!" she almost screamed.

"I am so sorry Jane, look, I just need to get into Lawson's office, when I get all the files, I promise I will be gone, but I can lock up, no one will know. Please Jane". He pleaded.

"Jamie, I really shouldn't leave you here alone, but…but I will leave you my keys, when you have the files lock up Mr Lawson's office and put the keys in my bottom draw under the black file and you are to keep this our little secret, cause if Mr Lawson finds out, I will loose my job and so will you!" she said.

"I absolutely agree Jane, I don't want to loose my job either, you're secret is safe with me, just between the two of us. I get it." he said. Jane unlocked the office and passed Jamie the keys.

"Remember what I said Jamie, or I will hunt you down!" she growled.

"Now go Jane, before you're late for, where did you say you were going?"

"Oh never mind, just say nothing…understand!" she called back over her shoulder as she rushed to the elevator.

Jamie stood at the door listening for the "ding" of the elevator, he heard the doors open and close. Smiling he said, "Now for Plan A".

Chapter Nine

Jamie knew that the Friday night meetings always finished around six thirty; it was now three minutes after five. He went in to Lawson's office with Jane's keys in his hot little hands. He knew Lawson always kept his briefcase locked in his bottom draw, he tried 3 keys before he heard the click of the lock. Placing the briefcase on the desk he opened it and there in the top was the pass card. He put everything back in place in case someone came to the office unexpectedly.

The pass card was the only way down to the vault floor and only the three partners had one. Jamie knew Lawson's pass code, him and his wife's birthdays', how original he thought. God bless Jane's little secret book hidden in her desk. He had searched for and found it one night after working late as he needed information to make his plan a success. He had hidden his sports bag in the men's room opposite the elevator, before he ran up to Jane.

Jamie entered the elevator with his bag and swiped the pass card, as the doors closed he took out the New York Yankees' jacket and baseball cap and put them on for the camera. He waited and watched as the elevator dissented to the seventh floor and his $4 million.

The elevator doors opened, in front of Jamie was a huge steel barred door. It reminded him of a jail cell. He swiped the pass card and punched in the code, the door clanged and slid open. He stepped inside, there was another barred door this time he swiped the card, the door would only open when an account number was entered in. Jamie punched in his account number, the door swung open and he stepped in to the vault.

He knew he only had a minimal window of opportunity and checked his watch, he had to move quickly. On the left side were safety deposit boxes, on the right side, were shelves stacked with cash, all neat in their bundles and denominations.

Jamie opened the sports bag and stacked in as much as possible. He made sure he left room at the top to fit in his jacket and cap and enough room for his squash racket to protrude. Before he knew it, he was back in the elevator on his way to Lawson's office. He removed the jacket and cap and stuffed them into the sports bag.

He had left the vault in plenty of time as it was programmed to close and lock at exactly six o'clock. He knew that Lawson would be back in his office around six or six thirty. Jamie returned to Lawson's office, on the way past he hid the sports bag behind the partition and went to the office door, he looked down and froze; there was light coming from under the door. Had he left a light on? he couldn't remember. He tried to think of something to say in case Roderick Lawson was back early. He knocked on the door then tried the handle, it didn't move, it was still locked. He unlocked the door and hurried to the desk to put the pass card back in the brief case before wiping it clean. As he was locking the draw he heard the sound of the elevator, he checked his watch, it was only eight minutes to six.

"Yes, that will be fine Simon, I can have those papers for you by, say, Tuesday or Wednesday next week. I can get Jane to print out the contracts and get them sent over to you." said Lawson, speaking into his cell.

"Right, that's no problem,"

Chapter Ten

Jamie quickly and quietly locked the door behind him and placed the keys carefully in Jane's draw. Jamie crept down the hallway and spotted Lawson standing outside the elevator still speaking on his cell phone. He went back, picked up the bag and crawled under the workstation in the corner of the office, behind the partition. Lawson went past him and into his office. The meeting had finished early. Jamie knew he couldn't leave with him in his office, as he would hear the sound from the elevator. He knew he couldn't carry the bag down the fire exit, he would just have to wait for Lawson to leave. Jamie's legs were starting to cramp as he had them tucked up under his chin with the bag jammed in behind him. He stayed there for almost twenty five minutes. Then finally Roderick Lawson turned off the lights and locked his office, left and took the elevator to the basement car park.

Jamie crawled out from under the desk and stretched his legs and rubbed them as they were starting to get pins and needles. He quietly walked to the elevator and waited until it had reached the basement car park. He waited for a short time. Then he pressed the button. Down in the car park there were only a few cars left, Jamie threw the bag in the back seat and drove out.

"Hey Jamie, big weekend planned?" asked Tony the security guard.

"Nah, same ole, same ole, you?" replied Jamie.

"Same ole, same ole, going to squash tonight?' he asked, noticing the sports bag and squash racquet in the back seat.

"Yeah, have to keep fit" said Jamie.

"Have a good one, see ya Monday" he smiled.

"Yep, see ya Monday" smiled Jamie, as he drove out into the street.

"See ya Monday….not goddam likely". Jamie said out loud to himself as he drove down the Wall Street block for the last time. He laughed and laughed again.

Chapter Eleven

Lenny was looking forward to the visit. It was Friday night and his friend was coming over. Jamie had time for Lenny, not because he felt sorry for him, but because they were pals.

Lenny tided up the apartment as best he could; he took a shower, shaved and even washed his hair. Jamie would be there around nine, so he decided to make himself a sandwich and cup of coffee, as it was only seven o'clock. Lenny turned on the TV and watched Wheel of Fortune his favourite show. He got tired easily these days, so after his show finished he decided to have a nap as he tired easily these colder days. He wondered what they would do tonight, maybe would catch a movie, or go to a bar, he didn't mind. It was getting cold out now so maybe they would just get pizza and a couple of six-packs and talk about old times.

Lenny hated winter he always got sick, since the accident his body couldn't fight off the germs like he used to. He always spent as much time in his apartment as possible getting his medications and stocking up on food so he didn't have to go out in the cold.

Chapter Twelve

Jamie drove home very carefully, he had a precious cargo on the back seat and he wasn't taking any chances. He arrived back at his apartment and parked his car down in the underground car park. He left his coat on the passenger seat, removed the bag from the car and locked it.

Up in his apartment he locked the door behind him, feeling a little bit paranoid. He took out the army surplus duffel bag and old clothes that he had collected. He took the black garbage bags from under the sink and began to put the bundles of money in the bags, seal and tape them, he didn't bother to count the money, he knew how much he took . He pushed the money bundles down into the bottom of the bag then he took some clothes and packed them on top. Changed his suit and left it on the floor of his bedroom. He changed into the old clothes leaving all his good suits and clothes in the closet and drawers.

He made a cup of coffee and left it on the kitchen counter untouched. He took a bite out of a cookie and left it beside the cup. He unlocked the door to his terrace and left it opened a few inches. He knocked over the coffee table, breaking the lamp and threw some sofa cushions on the floor, his cell phone and wallet and messed up the rug.

He looked out of the peep hole in the door, the hall was empty, leaving his keys inside on the table next to the door, he slipped into the hall and made his way to the Fire Exit stairwell. The exit opened on to the alley be side his building. He pulled his baseball cap down over his face and made his way down to the subway and took the train down to the docks and Lenny.

Chapter Thirteen

A chilling wind blew, sending the bitter icy air through Jamie's body. Discarded paper, rubbish and leaves rustled along the sidewalk unseen in the darkness of the cold deserted street.

The old apartment block was only a short distance away and Jamie knew he would be safe. Lenny opened the door; first he saw Jamie, then the duffel bag.

"Hey Lenny, how ya doin?"

"O-okay, you g-goin somewhere?" asked Lenny

"No, but I was wondering if it would be alright for me to bunk on your couch for

a while, I think I need to tell you the truth."

Jamie sat down on the sofa and told Lenny that he had lost his job, that he was behind in the rent and needed somewhere to stay until he found a job and would it be ok.

"Sure i-is, like r-r-roomies in c-college" stammered Lenny, excited.

"How about a beer pal, just like college" said Jamie pulling out a six-pack.

Lenny was glad of the company on a Friday night, but now he would have company all the time, Jamie was his friend and was happy for him to stay as long as he wanted, after all they were buddies and buddies help each other.

"Hey how about we go get some more beer and maybe a pizza, I'm getting hungry"

" I have something for you; I know you are a big New York Yankee's fan, so here you go". Jamie pulled out the Yankee's jacket and cap and gave it to Lenny.

His eyes watered up a little as he took the jacket and put it on. No one had given him a gift in a very long time.

"Th-thank you Jamie, its great. I l-love it" said Lenny a little choked up.

"That's ok, I know you were a fan, and I don't wear them anymore, so I thought you might like it, don't forget the cap."

They walked up the street to the pizzeria' Lenny in his new jacket and cap, Jamie in Lennys' old army coat and cap. Lenny didn't stop smiling all night, he even slept in the jacket and cap. Jamie was pleased that he could give Lenny such a small gift but it meant so much to him.

Chapter Fourteen

The FBI had been called in to help the New York Police Department investigate the multi million dollar theft. All the partners agreed that Jamie Blake must have been forced into committing the robbery.

They all spoke highly of him, even though he had been passed over a few times for promotions, they still felt he was innocent.

Karl DeWitt and Morgan Moxham, were assigned to the case. After speaking with the partners, they searched Blake's desk and took away his computer.

They then moved to search his apartment. Entering the apartment with a key from the complex manager. The manager told them that he was a quiet guy, never had any problems with him; he was a friendly fellow, polite, always paid his rent, no noisy parties, all in all a good tenant.

As they entered, DeWitt noticed the keys on the stand next to the door, "Looks like, wherever he was going he didn't need keys"

Moxham nodded and looked around the room. "I'd better check the terrace; doors are opened for a reason." He moved carefully across the room and on to the terrace. Nothing out of place.

DeWitt walked into the bedroom, he noticed the clothes on the floor, he checked the closet and draws, all the clothes were still there. He checked the bathroom cabinet, toothbrush and toothpaste still there, shaving cream and razor, some hair products, Tylenol, nothing seemed to be missing. He walked back out into the main room then into the kitchen.

"Coffee cup is full, looks like he didn't have a chance to drink it.

"Yeah, I saw that, there's nothing much in the fridge, but that could be because he was a guy living on his own, who didn't like going to the market, maybe he did takeaway most nights" said Moxham. "Anything in the bin?"

"Not much, burger wrappers, takeaway containers that's all"

"What do you make of the mess in here" he said, pointing to the over turned coffee table and sofa cushions scattered over the floor the broken lamp, cell phone.

"Looks to me like where ever they wanted him to go, he wasn't to keen on going"

"Better get Forensics in here, see if they can come up with something, but a job this big, they would have every angle covered, I don't think they'll find much. Oh and they had better get the car towed over to the lab from the basement, you never know, they may have left us a clue."

"See if the Tech guys can come up with something on his cell phone" said Moxham. But they knew this was a professional gang and knew what they were doing. They got word that the hard dive from Blake's computer had been removed, but they were still working on it.

Chapter Fifteen

Winter came with a vengeance the wind cutting through the streets like an icy razor, the snow fell heavily and covered the streets, the cars pushing the dirty white slush against the sidewalk mixed with rubbish.

Lenny caught a bad case of flu, Jamie bought him medication that made him sleepy, cooked all the meals, did the shopping and laundry, and made sure Lenny was comfortable. He even bought a heater for the apartment.

Every morning Jamie went down to the corner and bought the newspaper so Lenny could read his favourites, the funnies and the shipping news.

Jamie scanned the papers to see what the FBI and the police were doing and where they were in their hunt for the fugitive. At first there were sightings of him at the airport, train stations and borders. The best lead they had was a Canadian Border Patrol Officer, reported seeing a man matching Blake's description crossing the boarder into Canada, in the company of three men of Latino appearance

They were driving a gold Lincoln Town Car. They said their papers seemed to be in order, but feel now that they may have been forgeries'. Jamie read how the FBI agents had flown to Canada to meet with law enforcement. On most days now, just a few lines on a page now and then, but that suited Jamie just fine. Jamie would search the Employment section and pretend to look for a job.

Lenny was starting to feel much better. His flu symptoms had just about gone and he was feeling stronger. Jamie insisted he still stay indoors for a while, just to be on the safe side. Lenny was touched that Jamie cared for him and had taken such good care of him all winter.

"That's what friends are for" replied Jamie, when Lenny thanked him.

One morning as Jamie came out of the shower, Lenny was excited.

"J-Jamie l-l-look….they want d-deckhands, f-f-for an I-Italian f-f-freighter"

He shoved the paper into Jamie's hands.

"Ok..Ok..I'll go down and see about it, it's too cold for you to go, I don't want you to get sick and not be able to get a job." said Jamie.

Later that day he went down to see the Dock Master, he walked into the office, there was a small Chinese girl with long dark hair sitting behind the counter, he told her he was there about the deckhand jobs.

"Just take a seat and I will let Mr. Shepard know you're here" she said, picking up the phone. A short time later a large man with a barrel chest and greying hair came out of the adjoining office.

He shook Jamie's hand, he had a strong grip with large calloused hands.

"Come on through" he motioned to Jamie. He gave him a run down on the job, he explained that he needed a current passport and that he would contact him later in the week. Jamie told him he would be back with the passport.

Back at the apartment Jamie told Lenny about the meeting and said he had to have his passport ready, in case they got the jobs. They went through Lenny's apartment and in an old tin box they found Lenny's passport some papers and his birth certificate. The passport was almost expired, so Jamie told him he would go up town to get renewed.

Chapter Sixteen

Jamie knew the office closed at four thirty, so he waited until four ten then walked to the counter. The clerk looked at the clock then at Jamie.

"Can I help you Sir," he asked, glancing at the clock again.

"I need my passport renewed."

The clerk handed him some forms and asked for them to be filled out.

Jamie took his time as the clerk watched the clock.

"May I help you with the forms Sir, and do you have your birth certificate with you?" he asked, clearly irritated.

Jamie handed him the forms and the clerk fired questions at him and ticked boxes and wrote the answers quickly. It was almost four twenty five when he punched the information into the computer and waited until the machine next to him slipped out the new page with the picture. He transferred the new page into the passport with swift efficiency still keeping an eye on the clock. By four thirty five, Jamie walked out with the renewed passport in his pocket and a smile on his face.

Jamie then went on to the library, amazing what you can do on the internet. He printed out all the paperwork he needed. Then on to the bank for that new account.

Lenny waited for him to return; he looked at his new passport and thanked Jamie for renewing it . Lenny didn't like going up town, so he was grateful he didn't have to go, he detested forms as he found them to hard to understand. But he knew Jamie would understand, he was smart and he was his buddy.

"No problem buddy, don't worry about it". said Jamie.

Later that week Jamie spoke to Mr. Shepherd, he told him that the ship was due in on Wednesday morning at eleven, and that it would sail out again on the following Tuesday morning. He told him they would get three days shore leave in Naples, once the ship had docked and been unloaded, then reloaded to return a few days later.

"Be here by six am sharp, the ship leaves on time, so don't be late."

Chapter Seventeen

On Monday night Jamie and Lenny had dinner early they needed a good nights sleep. They kept talking about what they could do and what they would see, and how excited they were to even think of getting any sleep. Jamie suggested they go get some beer and maybe a pizza for the last time.

As they walked up the street, Jamie started talking about Uncle Mike's building, they decided to go and see how the construction was coming along.

The gate was padlocked, but there was enough room for them to squeeze through. Lenny walked around telling Jamie what things were for. Jamie asked about the steel beams held in place by scaffolding, Lenny explained that the steel beams were put deep in a 40 foot hole and that the scaffolding would hold it in place while they poured the cement in to fill the hole and take the scaffolding down when it was dry and set. As Lenny stood looking into the hole, he didn't see Jamie take the piece of wood from the stack.

The wood made a loud clunking cracking sound as it crushed the back of Lenny's skull; his lifeless body fell into the hole. Jamie took a wheel barrow from the site and filled it with sand and gravel and poured it into the hole, it took five barrow loads to completely cover Lenny's body. He stood looking into the hole, tears running down his face.

He wiped the handles of the barrow and shovel and put them back where he found them. He looked around and slipped out of the gate and walked down the street, when he got to the corner he started to limp.

Chapter Eighteen

He had spent his last night in The Penthouse, he took one last look the following morning before he closed the door on his 'former life', he would disappear like the witness protection program, self inflicted of course he told himself.

At six on Tuesday morning Jamie stood on the bitter windy dock. There were three other men with him. George Shepherd came out of his office and checked their passports and papers.

He spoke to the leading ship hand and introduced the men. The ship was a transport carrier. He didn't know what they were taking back to Naples, but he didn't care either. Carlo was the leading ship hand, he took the men aboard the ship and showed them their cabins.

"This is where you'll be bunked" he said

"This is Vincent, he will be your cabin mate."

A tall dark haired man was pulling the covers up on his bunk, he stood up and

shook hands.

"Vincent will show you around, ask him anything if you're not sure, ok" he turned and left.

"You can stow your stuff here" pointing to a locker. "It has a padlock on the handle" he told him that everyone was responsible for their own stuff and to keep the key with him.

Jamie waited until Vincent left the cabin and opened the locker and took out some clothes and put them in the drawers next to his bunk, along with his toothbrush and shaving kit. He put the duffel bag in the locker and snapped the padlock shut, he hid the key in his sock.

Chapter Nineteen

Vincent came back and took him to the galley for some breakfast. Afterwards they went out on deck to prepare the ship to leave the dock.

Jamie thought to himself as he worked, thank god Lenny had all those books on these ships and how everything worked. Jamie would wait until Lenny was sleeping and then study all he could on the running of these freighters and deckhand duties.

He had familiarised himself with the ship lingo and what everything meant. He studied how most of the mechanical equipment was used and what its function was. He had done alright so far, answered most of the questions pretty easily.

At eleven am sharp the captain started the enormous engines, the dock workers removed the giant ropes and the deckhands pulled them up to the ship and wrapped them around large metal rollers and pulled the switch to wind them in.

Jamie was told to go to the bow of the ship and hose down the mud from the chain and the anchor, he went over to inspect that there was nothing that would get caught.

The huge anchor chain started to rewind, slowly grinding its way up the side of the ship, it scarped loudly against the metal as it came to its resting place. Jamie pulled the brake lever to keep it in place during the voyage across the ocean to Italy. He had never been there before but he couldn't resist the little farm house he had seen on the internet and thanks to Lenny's passport and birth certificate he was able to open a bank account and wire the money transfer to secure the property in the Tuscan hills

He was pleased with himself, so far, so good.

Chapter Twenty

The Chino slowly sailed down the harbour, leaving the polluted water churning in its wake. The New York skyline looked beautiful against the blue sky, it was a beautiful sunny day, even for the lousy winter it had been.

What a send off he thought to himself. Jamie made his way to the bow of the ship and lit a cigarette. He sat on the deck and peered intently and managed to catch a glimpse of The Penthouse, between the tall buildings surrounding the docks. He smiled to himself and stood up, moving to the side of the ship he leaned over and flicked the cigarette butt into the harbour water below.

His eyes traced along the skyline picking out buildings he knew. He could now see Uncle Mike's construction site of the office block they were building.

"Bet you never thought you'd be helping to hold up a forty story building did you my old pal?" he said.

He felt the pang of regret in his chest; he knew deep down in his soul, he couldn't have left Lenny alone again to live in that ghetto. He knew he had no choice, he couldn't take him with him, he would never have survived the trip or the hard work expected of him aboard the ship.

Besides he was in a better place now with his mom and dad, he would be happy being with them again, he rationalised to himself, as a tear escaped the corner of his eye. He knew Lenny was his best friend and he would miss him.

"Good bye Lenny and thanks for everything, especially being such a pal."

Chapter Twenty One

The ship sailed on past the statue of Liberty. Jamie raised his cap and said

"Good bye pretty lady, keep America safe, 'cause I won't be back for a long time."

He thought about the FBI agent's who were trailing him throughout Canada, wondering where they would go next. He had outsmarted them all by staying in New York, right under their noses, so to speak. After all, who would think of looking for someone with millions of dollars for an escape, would be still in the same city and a ghetto no less. His plan had worked out, better than he had hoped. When ever he visited Lenny, he would always park his car at least two or three blocks away and walk.

He had given Lenny the Yankee's jacket and cap, so he would have to wear Lenny's old army coat and battered cap. He make sure that each time he left the apartment in the daytime, he did so alone, always telling Lenny he should rest and that he didn't mind. When buying the food or medicines, he would buy what he need for his 'trip' toothbrush, toothpaste, shaving kit, some books and put them in his duffel bag as Lenny slept. Whenever he stepped outside the apartment, he would limp. He grew his hair long and unkempt like Lenny's, he always pulled the scarf up around his face and his baseball cap pulled down, most of all he limped.

The language would be no barrier as he had taken Italian in college thanks to the huge crush he had on Maria Capinola .

He had fooled everyone, from Joe the paper guy, always saying.

"How ya doin Lenny, cold enough for ya." Jamie would just nod.

Stella the waitress, even Frankie in the Pizza shop, everyone called him Lenny. He even fooled old Mrs. O'Riley the Irish widow from down stairs, who always spoke to Lenny about her son, who lived in Connecticut and never had time to visit her.

But sadly it just proved that Lenny was nothing to these people, just a poor guy in an old army coat and battered baseball cap. How very sad he thought.

Chapter Twenty Two

"Hey, hey Lenny". called Vincent. "Chow time" he called and waved his hand

"Be right there," said Jamie.

He stood close to the rail and watched the New York city skyline fade into the distance.

Everything had so far gone to plan, after the ship docks in Naples and the ship had been unloaded, he would take his three day shore leave.

He had done his research carefully. The train would take him to Rome, then north to Tuscany. A short drive 30miles to the farm house, his new home.

His old life was fading away over the water, but he knew his new life awaited him. He could feel excitement and regret churn inside his chest. He knew he would never forget Lenny because without him none of this would have been possible.

He tipped his cap and said goodbye to Lenny and the Whiz Kid of Wall Street for the last time.

JULIA'S STORY

Chapter One

She was packed and ready to go, her suitcase sat in the hallway near the front door, it was only 7.15, he would pick her up at 9. Her new life was to begin tonight. She tried to stay calm but she couldn't, she paced around the sitting room and checked herself in the mirror more times than she could count. She wanted to look perfect for him, for tonight they would elope and she would wake up next to him for the first time, as husband and wife. She wished her mother had lived long enough to meet Robbie. She had lost her father at the age of 11 and her mother had past away only 6months ago. She had been lost and alone, until she met Robbie. She sat down on the sofa and closed her eyes, remembering how she met him.

"Come on Julia….it will be fun…you know you can't stay here in this house forever, your mum wouldn't have wanted that for you" cried Marcie.

Julia knew she was right,

"But how can I go, it's a Methodist Dance for gods' sake"

"Well you will just have to swap religions for one night! I am sure God will forgive you".

Julia was smiling the temptation was so great, she gave in to it. "Ok….but what if someone asks me…do I say I am Catholic…or Methodist?"

"Methodist! You ninny." said Marcie.

They both laughed at each other.

"Ok, I will come by at 7 tonight, so be ready"

"Seven. Gotcha."

Chapter Two

The dance was very exciting and fun, the music, the laughter the people. Julia thought maybe she could swap religions for good!

But, no she was christened Catholic, just like her mum and dad and her faith was too strong to leave for good, she knew that in her heart. But one night was ok.

"Excuse me, would you like to dance?"

Julia turned, and there in front of her stood the boy she had seen standing across the room speaking to the Methodist Minister. She had noticed him just after they arrived, he was very cute.

"Well, err. Yes,"

He took her hand and led her out onto the floor, at first she was embarrassed and didn't know quite where to look. He just smiled at her.

"I've not seen you at any of our dances before, are you new in the village?" he asked.

"No." she said. Not knowing what to say. "I just don't go to many dances". she offered.

"Well, I am glad you came to this one, we don't get anyone half as pretty as you."

She could feel the blood rush to her face and she blushed.

He gave a little laugh.

"Pretty and modest as well" he joked.

"So how about we introduce ourselves, my name is Robbie Compton, and my dad is the Minister." Julia looked at him, trying to stay calm

"Your dad, he's the Minister".

"Is that a problem?" Robbie asked.

"No, no, not at all." she said.

"I'm Julia, Julia Reeve."

"Very pleased to meet you, Julia Reeve" he said and bowed

slightly.

Julia didn't know what to do, he was talking to her, but her mind was going a hundred miles an hour. How could she tell him she was there under false pretences? Methodists only mixed with Methodists, not Catholics.

One dance turned into another, she never wanted the night to end, just to be in his arms was enough, she felt like Cinderella. She knew that when he found out about her, she would never see him again so she was content to have this one night. She had never felt this way about anyone, her emotions came as a bit of a surprise to her. She felt excitement, elated and confused, all at the same time. Was this normal when you liked someone she thought. How odd.

Chapter Three

Two days after the dance she still couldn't get Robbie out of her mind. Marcie rang the doorbell.

"You'll never guess!!!"

"Guess what?" asked Julia.

"Robbie Compton!" she exclaimed.

"What about him?"

"He rang me and asked for your phone number!" cried Marcie.

"My... phone number?" she asked surprised.

"Yes… and I told him, so he is going to ring you for sure!" she was more excited than Julia.

"Oh my god, what will I say to him, I can't go on lying to him Marcie, what do I do?"

"You're asking me! I'm the one who told you to fib in the first place!"

"Ok, if I am going to have any chance with this guy, I will have to be honest, and tell him the truth, if he goes, then my conscience is clear, if he stays, well…god what do I do?"

Marcie left her to think, Julia's head was spinning…

"Do I do the right thing, or do I risk losing him?" she asked herself.

The ringing of the hall phone interrupted her train of thought.

"Hello?" she said. Annoyed.

"Hello, Julia? This is Robbie, Robbie Compton, from the dance, how are you?"

"Fine" she answered.

"I was wondering if you would like to go to the cinema on Friday night?"

She froze on the spot, her hands shaking. "Yes, that would be very nice" she managed to say.

"Brilliant, I have your address. Marcie gave it to me with

your number. I'll pick you up at 6.30pm sharp, see you then" he rung off.

"Oh my god" she whispered.

The sound of a car jilted her out of her daydream, she sat up and ran to the window, but the car drove on down the street. She looked at her watch it was just before 8pm. She went into the kitchen and made herself a cup of Chamomile tea to sooth her nerves. Back in the sitting room looking out the window the street was in darkness except for the soft yellowish glow of the streetlights reflected on the damp road.

She settled back on the sofa sipping her tea, she leaned back and closed her eyes.

"Now, where was I, ah yes, our first date?" she said to herself out loud.

When he had arrived, Julia took him into the sitting room and told him about Marcie talking her into going to the dance, that she was Catholic and wouldn't change that and she was sorry to have given him a false impression. He had sat and listened to her, nodded occasionally and said, "I see" a few times.

Then he stood up and said "So, we had better get going, don't want to miss the cinema!"

Chapter Four

She looked at him, confused "So you don't mind, you understand?"

"Look Julia, my father is a Minister, that's his life and his choice, it's not mine. People have their own religion, and I respect that. But I have to tell you, that my parents wouldn't take to me dating a Catholic."

"I see," she said, willing herself not to cry. She kept her eyes on the floor, not daring to look into his eyes, those beautiful blue eyes.

"It will be tricky, but I think we can pull it off!"

"Tricky?" she said, looking at him surprised.

"You mean you still want to see me?"

"You bet, if you want to that is?"

"Oh yes, I do I do..!" she couldn't stop the tears this time.

They had continued to see each other in secret; Robbie would park his car in the back lane and come in via the back door. She understood the need for them to keep it quiet, as Robbie didn't want to upset his parents. They would need time to adjust, after all a young Methodist boy should marry a young Methodist girl. It was the way they were raised and their beliefs were still strong, although, out of touch with today's society. But their need to be together always was too strong to ignore any longer, and Robbie had gotten down on one knee.

"I know we have only known each other for just over 4 months, but I love you Julia, I want to spend the rest of my life with you and I don't care what my parents think. I want you to be my wife and have lots of children with you. I love you more than I thought was possible, please Julia, marry me!"

She looked down at him, into his sparkling blue eyes, his strong jaw, his dark messy hair, he was smiling and anxious, she knew she loved him just as much.

"Of course I'll marry you, I love you so very much Robbie!"

He stood and took her into his arms and kissed her all over her face and neck and she took his hand and led him upstairs to her room.

Chapter Five

She opened her eyes and looked at the clock, it was 8.55pm, only 5 more minutes and he would be there to take her away. She looked down and patted her stomach gently, she had been to the doctors earlier that day. He had confirmed what she knew in her heart. She was pregnant with Robbie's child, but she had decided to tell him after the ceremony, she would not let Robbie marry her if he felt he had to. This would be her gift to him on their wedding day.

She went into the kitchen and washed out her cup and put it away. She took a last look around the room, her last time as a single woman. She checked her watch, it was 9.00pm at last.

Standing at the sitting room window she knew he would be there any minute, she started to smile, then let out a little giggle, it seemed her whole body was trembling with excitement.

"Get a hold of your self girl!" she scorned herself, but still smiling.

But she couldn't contain her excitement; she went to the mirror near the front door and looked at herself one more time. In her reflection she saw how her eyes sparkled she was so happy and she knew that she would look into Robbie's eyes and see the same thing. A car approached but kept on going.

"Come on Robbie, my darling, hurry." she said into the darken street.

Looking out of the window again, she had turned off all the lights and stood in the dark, waiting. Five minutes turned into fifteen minutes, then fifteen into thirty minutes.

"It's ok, so he is running a bit late, he must be getting petrol, yes, that's what it is" she told herself. It was almost ten thirty, she had gone into the kitchen to make herself another cup of tea she didn't hear the car pull up. There was the knock at the door. Julia almost dropped the tea cup.

"Robbie…at last I was so..!" she said as she opened the

door.

She stopped herself when she saw James, Robbie's brother standing on the doorstep, his eyes red and swollen.

"James, what are you doing here?" she asked, trying to control herself.

"Its Robbie," he sniffed.

"What about Robbie?" she said, panic starting to rise in her voice.

"There was an accident, with a lorry, I'm so very sorry, Robbie was taken to the hospital, I spoke to him before they took him into the operating theatre, he told me to tell you to come to the hospital, but he died on the table.

So I came to tell you first. I though you should know... I'm sorry Julia, but I have to go, you know, other people to inform." and he was gone.

Her life ended there on the doorstep, the pain gripped her whole body, she closed the door and the darkness enveloped her.

Chapter Six

"It's just the shock, the baby seems fine, we have given you something for the pain and the spotting has stopped, maybe you can go home in the morning," said the doctor.

Julia lay back in the hospital bed, she was numb. How could this happen, she thought to her self. Why is it that everyone I love is taken away from me? What is it that I have done so wrong? Turning her face into the pillow she sobbed until she had no tears left and slept.

The taxi pulled up out the front of her house, she looked at the door and knew she could no longer stay there.

"Can you wait for me, I will just be a few minutes." she asked the driver

"Yes, take your time I'll wait, where do you want to go from here?" he asked.

"The train station" she answered, without even thinking.

"Right you are then miss."

Julia opened the door and stepped inside, the house felt cold and empty, she wanted to run from here as far away as she could, away from the hurt and the heartache she felt burning into her body.

Upstairs she gathered her belonging, bank books, cash and papers. She phoned the Realtor and went back down stairs; she picked up her suitcase and walked out the front door without a backward glance. She dropped the house keys under the mat and climbed into the taxi.

Chapter Seven

The train to London was on time. It would be a good two hour journey, buying the London Times she would look for a place to live. She had enough money with her to stay in a cheap lodging for a week or more. She would have to find something soon but she had her savings to live on until the sale of the house came through. Julia circled a few one bedroom flats and a couple of bed sitters that sounded reasonable and furnished.

Arriving at Charring Cross station she made her way up from the underground to the street. People were rushing about, traffic fumes, noise and the heat made her feel sick and light headed. Julia walked down towards Covent Garden where she found a Coffee shop and went in. She sat back in a comfortable chair and realized that she hadn't eaten since, she couldn't remember when, so much had happened in the last 24 hours.

"Can I get you something luv?" asked the waitress, smiling down at her. "You look like you're all done in, ya poor luv, how 'bout a sandwich and a nice cup of tea?" she asked.

Julia wasn't hungry, but knew she had to eat, she had to think of the baby now, not just her.

At least she had part of Robbie that no one could take from her, and she was determined to keep it safe.

Chapter Eight

With a little luck later that day she had found a small furnished bed sit that she could afford. She would stay there until the baby was born, then find something bigger. Julia applied for a cashier's job at a small supermarket nearby and stayed till she could no longer drag herself to work; the long hours standing day after day took their toll on her.

She went to the clinic for regular checkups and a week before the birth she was admitted to hospital for rest as her blood pressure was far too high. Julia kept to herself. Her nurse Sally would come and chat with her most days as she had noticed that no one came to visit Julia or make any phone inquiry about her health. They became quite close and often Sally would stop in on her after her shift had finished. One morning Sally stopped by her room and she was gone.

"Julia has gone down to delivery, why don't you go and check on her, its pretty quiet at the moment." said Jane the head nurse.

"Thanks Jane, I will." said Sally already on her way to the lift.

Sally arrived just in time to help with the birth. She held Julia's hand and helped her through the birth.

"She's lovely and healthy too" said the midwife.

"Well done!" said Sally smiling. "She is beautiful."

"Thanks Sally, I couldn't have done it without you" said Julia breathlessly, and closed her eyes, she was exhausted.

Julia woke a few hours later with Sally sitting beside her bed nursing the precious bundle.

She was singing a lullaby to the baby ever so softly

"Is she alright?"

"She is brilliant, so sweet and peaceful" answered Sally quietly.

Julia took the baby from Sally, undid her nightdress, put the baby to her breast and fed her. She felt happy and at peace for the first time in many months.

Julia called her little girl Angelique Rose.

Chapter Nine

On the fourth day Julia told Sally about finding a place to live as her lease had expired on the bed sit. Sally told her not to worry and that she would help her.

"Well, things seem to be going well with you, baby is feeding well and she is healthy, I think you can go home tomorrow" said Doctor Travis.

Home thought Julia…where would home be?

Sally came in to take her blood pressure and temperature, noticing Julia's sullen face she asked. "Hey why so glum, you can go home tomorrow".

"Yes" said Julia, "but home to where, my lease has expired and I have nowhere to take her home to!" Julia looked at the baby lying asleep in the crib beside her.

"Look" said Sally, taking a deep breath. "I know we haven't known each other very long, but I live on my own, the house is way too big for me since my parents passed away and I would love some company to come home to at night, and you can have your own room and we can both take care of the baby, so, what do you say? Will you at least think about it? Please".

"I will Sally, thank you." said Julia.

Sally left her to think, Julia knew that it would solve her problem of lodgings for the time being, at least until she found something else and having Sally around would be good in case anything happened with the baby, and Sally seemed very genuine so she decided to accept.

Sally arrived the next morning to pick them up. She had borrowed a car carrier for the drive home and a crib from a friend. Julia carried the baby out into the sunshine, she could feel the warmth against her skin and the soft blue sky was radiant. She hadn't felt the sun for over two weeks and it was glorious. Sally drove extra careful, a little too careful, thought Julia, but she didn't complain, it was good to be out in the fresh air again enjoying the outside. Sally turned into a beautiful tree lined street, the houses were all well cared for and the gardens groomed and neat. She turned into a pebbled driveway leading to a two story Tudor styled house. Julia could hardly believe it she had always loved the Tudor style houses, but never dreamed she would actually live in one.

Chapter Ten

After feeding and settling the baby down, Sally made them both a cup of tea and showed Julia around the rest of the house. It was larger than she imagined, four bedrooms, the fourth one turned into a library. There was a conservatorium off the kitchen where she and Sally ate breakfast in the morning sun. Sally had three days off so they shopped for food and things for the baby then she would have everything she needed when Sally was at work.

Sally and Julia were sitting in the parlor one evening after dinner, she had made them both a drink, then she asked. "Julia, you have never spoken about the baby's father, but it has been two months since you had her, do you think he should be told. I know it's none of my business, but if you ever want to talk, I am a really good listener."

"I think it's about time I did talk about it, I have had it bottled up inside me for so long, maybe you should know, who knows, it maybe good for me to get it off my chest." said Julia.

She told her the sad story of what had happened that night.

Sally sat and listened, she could feel the sadness and great loss Julia suffered. As Julia spoke the tears ran down her cheeks, and before she knew it Sally was crying to. They both decided to put the past behind them and to give the baby the best upbringing they could give her.

Chapter Eleven

The sale of the house in Willowmead finally came through and Julia could now pay her share of the expenses which eased her mind considerably.

"I think its time to celebrate your sale, so to hell with the tea, this calls for something stronger, what do you say to a glass of my twelve year old scotch?" said Sally.

"Perfect" smiled Julia. They toasted to the sale of the house, to the baby's health and to a new beginning and anything else they could toast to. It was the first time Julia had really laughed in a very long time.

After quiet a few scotches and toasts, they decided to head off to bed. The loud creaking of the bottom step made them both start to giggle uncontrollably.

"Sshhhh….you'll wake the baby" said Sally trying to regain some form of control.

They crept up the staircase and the even louder creaking of the top step had them in fits of laughter. Julia sneaked a look in on Angie, she was sleeping soundly. Sally said goodnight and staggered on down the hall to her room. Julia went to bed dreading the morning hangover.

He stood and watched as the lights in the house went out one by one. Then he crossed the road and headed towards the back lane in the dark.

Chapter Twelve

At six a.m. Julia woke to Angie crying, she dragged herself in to feed her. She had just settled the baby back into her cot when Sally peeked in the nursery.

"Coffee…?" said Julia.

"Yes please….very strong…very hot!!" said Sally.

Sally went off to the bathroom to brush her teeth and rinse the disgusting taste from her mouth, she had just finished when she heard the smashing of the cups.

"S-Sally." Julia called from the kitchen

Sally ran down stairs, she could hear the fear in Julia's voice, as she reached the kitchen; Julia was standing leaning against the bench, the look of terror in her eyes.

"Julia, what is it…what's wrong?"

Julia just lifted her hand and pointed to the table. Sally followed her gaze, she looked and on the table was a newspaper. It was the Willowmead Times, on the front page, the story of Robbie's accident and a picture of the crash scene.

Sally looked at a stunned Julia.

"How did this get here? Where did it come from?" asked Sally

"Julia..! Julia answer me, did you have this paper?" asked Sally.

"No!" screamed Julia.

"It was on the table when I came down."

She looked at Sally

"Was it you did you put it there?"

"Me! How could I? you've only just told me about Robbie!"

They looked at each other unable to speak, then Sally went to the door of the conservatory, it was locked, they hadn't forgotten to lock it last night.

"From now on, we make sure the house is locked up, windows, doors, garage everything. Ok"

Julia just nodded Sally took the paper and threw it in the bin.

"Why would someone do this, what are they trying to do to me?" asked Julia

"Can you think of anyone that would try to harm you or who knew about you and Robbie?" said Sally

"No one knew about us, I never told anyone, not even Marcie, I just told her it didn't work out between us, and Robbie told no one we promised each other we wouldn't."

They sat at the table and drank their tea not saying anything just trying to think.

He was back again that night, he knew she would be rattled by the paper. He stood in the dark at the laneway across the street, watching, waiting.

Soon my family will be with me, my family, mine.

Chapter Thirteen

"If only I could have been at the hospital, if only I had known, oh Robbie if only, if only". Julia put her head in her hands and sobbed, her body trembled, racked with pain and heartache, she thought the pain would never leave her, and now she was sure. The sound of the baby monitor, made her sit up, she wiped her face with her hands, threw the paper back into the bin and went upstairs.

Sally came home early, she had bought takeaway and a bottle of wine, as neither of them were in the mood to cook, they both knew they had to discuss what had happened and try to make some sort of sense of it.

"Is there anyone that you can think of in Willowmead that may have been told about you two or may have guessed?"

"No, I am sure of it."

"Why don't you call someone from the village, a friend, and see if they can shed some light on this"

"Ok, that's actually a good idea, just let me get my address book, I'll call Marcie, she was my good friend, I know she will tell me if she knows anything."

Julia dialed Marcie's number and spoke to her, she asked about Robbie, his family and friends, she explained to Marcie that she left in a hurry to look after a sick aunt, and that she would ring her again soon, that seemed to pacify Marcie on why she left so abruptly, she thanked her and hung up.

"Well, how did it go, did she know anything?" asked Sally anxiously.

"She filled me in on everything, she said that after Robbie's accident, about two months later Robbie's dad was sent to a new Parish up north near Newcastle and that no one had heard from them since. They took the accident very hard. His brother James started drinking very heavily, he got involved with a Spanish girl and she was pregnant, so they moved to Spain to be near her family. Apparently no one has heard from him either. It seems Robbie's accident destroyed their family. Marcie never knew about us, or even suspected."

"Well, someone knows something; I just wish I knew what their motives are." said Sally.

They were up against a brick wall, wondering who and why?

He was back again standing and watched from the laneway.

He would wait, it would take time, but she would understand once she realized the love was still there.

Chapter Fourteen

It was a cold Sunday afternoon, when Julia and Sally took Angelique to be christened. Light snowflakes covered the pathway to the old stone chapel.

The baby was wrapped in a shawl that Sally had been given by her mother.

It was the shawl Sally wore at her christening. After the ceremony they went to dinner and then home.

Julia fed and changed Angie, she was a beautiful little girl, she looked more and more like Robbie as she got older, but she still had Julia's nose and smile. It was hard to look at her and not remember Robbie.

Winter settled in and Christmas was around the corner. The excitement was building as Sally had bought just about every toy in the store. Sally stayed at home one afternoon with the baby while Julia went shopping on her own, she wanted to get Sally something special along with the bottle of 12 yr old scotch she wanted, as they had been through quite a few bottles since Julia moved in they were always finding an excuse to 'have a little drink!'

As Julia shopped she had the feeling she was being watched, she casually looked around every now and again, but decided she was being paranoid and continued her Christmas shopping before it got too late. Their first Christmas was a joyous occasion, as neither of them had family, they made it just the three of them and it was the best Christmas either of them had had in a long time.

Months passed and Angie was growing into a beautiful, intelligent little girl; It was soon her 1st birthday. One afternoon Sally took Angie shopping and Julia arrived home before them to wrap her gifts and hide them. As she approached the front door juggling the gifts, bags and keys she noticed a small package wrapped in pink paper, but no card. How odd she thought and took the parcel in with her. Julia had a strange feeling about the gift, so she opened it…inside was a pink cardigan with little purple flowers near the shoulders, as Julia unfolded it a small picture fell out. She picked it up and felt as if she had been struck! It was a picture of Julia and Robbie taken in a photo booth, on their first 'official' date. Julia had forgotten all about it. The shock of the picture made her lose all track of time, the next thing she heard was Sally's voice.

"Julia…Julia…are you alright. You look like you've seen a ghost!"

Sally looked at her then down at the picture in her hand.

"Oh my god….where did you get that?"

Julia couldn't speak, she just shook her head at Sally. "Stay here, I'll go and put Angie in her cot, now sit down ok. I'll be right back"

Sally picked up Angie and took her upstairs.

He just stood and watched, it was a long time before he could get back, things he had to do, but now he was back, watching his family, reminding her.

Chapter Fifteen

Julia couldn't believe it. It had been so long since anything like this had happened… who could be doing this…didn't they know how upsetting it would be! Sally came back and made her a cup of tea, and sat at the table and took Julia's hand.

"Do you have any idea who can be doing this? It's such a long time since anything like this has happened. I think maybe you should try and ring your friend again and see if she can shed some light on this."

"I know you are right, I will call tonight, maybe she can help."

After dinner that night Julia tucked Angie into bed and read her a story, she was asleep before the end. Julia kissed her, turned off the light and went down stairs.

Sally had poured her a drink and lit the fire which warmed the room and filled it with a soft glow. Julia picked up the phone and rang Marcie.

"Marcie? Its Julia, how are you?" said Julia.

"Julia, how lovely to hear from you, how are you?"

After some small talk Julia said.

"I was wondering if you had heard anything, about Robbie's family"

"Funny you should ask," replied Marcie.

Julia looked at Sally she could feel her heart beating faster.

"Why, what's happened?"

"Well, do you remember Jane Dawson from school? She works for the Bank of England and had to go to a conference in Spain. Anyway she met this Spanish fellow who told her that his sister had married an Englishman and that they had a little boy and that he had passed away with Leukemia, he said that it shattered his sister and that afterwards she and her husband had terrible rows because he blamed her for the boys death. Well it seems that she was very close to her family and that she had disappeared! The husband said that after a fight she packed her bags and left, he didn't tell anyone as he thought she went to her parents but after a week her parents went to see him and after finding out she had gone, reported it to the police who are still looking for her."

"What has that got to do with anything?"

"That's just it…the guy was Robbie's brother James!"

"Oh my God, is James still in Spain or did he come back to England?"

"Well apparently he was offered a job in Greece for some big construction company. The police had nothing on him so he left Spain and is now working for this company, he is very good with designing buildings or something they said."

"Did he ever come back home to England?" asked Julia

"No, he said that there was nothing back there for him and that's why he went to Greece, he said that there were more opportunities for him over there". said Marcie.

They chatted about mutual friends and gossip for a few more minutes then she said.

"Well thanks for that Marcie, say hello to your mum for me, we'll chat soon, bye".

Chapter Sixteen

They thought over what Marcie had told them and sat for awhile in silence sipping at their drinks.

"Maybe we are looking at this from the wrong angle. Maybe Robbie did tell someone about us and they are trying to rattle me for some reason, but why, who knows about Angie and why don't they just come to the door and speak to me?"

"They are just cowards" spat Sally.

"I know, you're right, only a coward would hurt someone and hide while they are terrorizing them"

"Gutless wonders, you know, we should fight back, they are trying to hurt you and keep you scared, well lets show this bastard that we aren't afraid, and the best way to do it is to live our lives as if nothing has happened, and the next time we find something, we will just throw it in the bin and not give them the satisfaction. Agreed?" said Sally.

"Agreed!" repeated Julia.

They shook hands and clinked glasses and with one swallow finished their scotches.

Julia decided it was time to find a job, she also realized that Angie needed to play and make friends with kids her own age.

"It will be good for her to be away from me for a change, wont it"?

"Yes of course, you're right she needs the company of other children, not just us old farts hanging around her all the time. It will give her a chance to grow and be independent, but how will you handle not being with her?"

Julia looked at Sally, and tears welled up in her eyes,

"Oh my god, I'm crying and I'm just talking about it"

"You're hopeless" laughed Sally.

"I know." she said half crying half laughing.

After numerous interviews, Julia finally secured a job as a receptionist at a Solicitors firm of Maddison, Davidson and

Peters.

She enjoyed the job and Angie had settled into her new day care without any trouble as she had a wonderful personality and everyone loved her.

Julia shared the receptionist duties with Becky Collins, who was a barrel of fun and always had things to tell Julia, she was very entertaining.

One morning Becky told Julia her brother Ben was coming to take her to lunch, she had some filing to do and asked Julia to buzz her when he arrived. A short time later as Julia was typing some correspondence, she looked up to see a very handsome solider standing at the desk.

"May I help you sir?" she said.

"Hi, I'm Ben, I was looking for my sister, Becky?"

"Sure, take a seat, I'll call her."

Julia buzzed Becky and she came straight out, she hugged Ben and gave him a kiss. He had returned from Iraq only a few weeks earlier.

"This is my big brother Ben" said Becky.

"How do you do" said Julia.

"I'm fine thanks Julia, its nice to meet you, Becky has told me she enjoys working with you" said Ben.

"The feeling is mutual, she's a good friend" smiled Julia.

"Well, we're off, lets go big brother, hope you are taking me somewhere expensive!" laughed Becky as she winked at Julia.

Ben opened the door for her and he looked back at Julia and said. "Maybe next time Julia, you can join us. It was a pleasure meeting you" he smiled and closed the door.

Julia's heart was pounding, she sat there staring at the door, wishing he would come back in and whisk her away, he was the most handsome man she had ever seen, and if she was invited to lunch with him she would definitely go!

Julia thought about him all the way home in the car. She picked up Angie, stopped at the shops and went home to prepare dinner. Angie sat at the table coloring in her favorite Little Mermaid book when the phone rang.

“Julia you will never guess“….gushed Sally. “Gilbert has asked me out to dinner and I said yes, I am so excited, I have admired him for so long and we get on so well, I just accepted at once.”

“That’s fantastic Sal, have a great time, oh and I won’t wait up.” Julia giggled!

“Wish me luck”

“You don’t need luck”

“Ok, bye” she rung off.

“Looks like it’s just you and me kid, Aunt Sally has a date” she said to Angie.

Chapter Seventeen

It had almost been 2 years since the last incident and Julia and Sally had kept their word and gone on with their lives. Sally had continued to see Gilbert, they had become engaged and the wedding wasn't far away. Julia had started seeing Ben, he was wonderful and a great influence on Angie, who loved him, especially when he wore his uniform! Everything had been booked, the church, the cars, and the reception house. Dresses were made, flowers and bouquets arranged, invitations send and accepted. The wedding was the next day, Sally and Julia sat on the sofa, just like they had done so many times before.

"You know, I am going to miss this, just sitting here chatting about everything and anything, drinking scotch with my best friend in the world, and you know Jools…you are my best friend in the world.!" smiled Sally.

"And you are mine, you saved my life, and Angie's"

"Yes, well you saved me from a lonely life in this big old house."

"I remember how lonely it was after Dad passed away, I nursed him here and in the hospital, he would say that the house had secrets, in the walls….I guess he meant that you know, that if these walls could talk as they say. Poor old fellow, he was just rambling in the end, I suppose it was the morphine and the pain, I was glad for him when he slipped away, very sad of course, but I knew he wouldn't be in any pain anymore, and I know Mum was waiting for him, that's what kept me sane" said Sally.

"Yes I remember when my Mum passed it is painful for those left behind. I still miss her you know, wish she could have seen Angie, I know she would have loved her."

"God, we are getting morbid, let's brighten up this conversation" laughed Sally.

"Right you are, well where are you going on your honeymoon?" asked Julia.

"I have no idea, but I know we will be away for at least 2 months, travelling around Europe, but Gil won't tell me, he wants it to be a surprise, but I will just have to ring and chat and make sure you're ok." laughed Sally.

"Don't worry, we will be alright, you will be on your honeymoon for heavens sake…so enjoy yourself and don't worry about us, besides Ben promised to keep a close eye on us."

"Well maybe I will sneak in a couple of calls to see how my two little darlings are going and all the gossip on that hunky Ben….oh you are a dark horse aren't you" Sally jibed.

Chapter Eighteen

The church bells rang out as Sally and Gilbert exchanged vows, it was a beautiful warm day even for the end of autumn, Gilbert had arranged for the release of 12 white doves and 50 white balloons as they stepped from the church. It was quite overwhelming and very romantic. Sally had a tear in her eye as she watched them float skyward. Angie in her little flower girls dress jumped and clapped her hands as she watched it all take place.

The reception went off without a hitch, everyone enjoyed themselves as the champagne flowed and everyone danced long into the night. At midnight a long white stretch limo pulled up outside the reception house and whisked the bride and groom away. Ben helped Julia load the wedding gifts into the car. They arrived home just after 1.30am. Ben carried Angie up the stairs and Julia undressed her and put her into bed, she was sound asleep and didn't wake up once.

"How about a night cap?" suggested Ben.

"Good thinking, thanks I'll have mine straight".

He poured the drinks while Julia slipped off her shoes and laid down on the sofa. He stoked the fire and added some more wood to warm the room. Julia took a sip of her scotch and let out a long sigh.

"I hope Sally is happy, no one deserves it more than her, she is such a great person, and I owe her my life."

"Judging by the look on their faces tonight, I would say they are very much in love and I am sure that Gil will take good care of her, he told me tonight that he was the happiest he had ever been and that Sally had made his life complete, sounds corny I know, but he was very sincere."

"I'm glad, I know Sally loves him, they will be fine",

Outside the night was becoming colder, the wind was stronger and fallen golden leaves blew along the street.

He stood watching the glow from the fire illuminating the front window.

Soon, my family, soon. He thought to himself, he smiled and dropped the cigarette to the ground and crushed it out in the snow.

Chapter Nineteen

Winter arrived swiftly with a vengeance, the sleet and snow falling much earlier than the previous years. Ben spent most of his time with Julia and Angie while Sally was still away. Angie had become good friends with a little girl named Tess and she had been invited to go on a long weekend trip to Tess' grandparent's house. They lived a good 3 hours away and Tess' mother Lisa and Julia had got along very well from the beginning. Angie begged Julia to let her go, and Julia didn't have the heart to say no.

So it was arranged that Tess' family would pick Angie up on Saturday morning around 7.30am. Angie was very excited, she and Julia had packed her bag the night before, she was awake by 6.30 and Julia made her breakfast, but she could only eat a small amount as she was just too excited. Tess and her parents arrived and Julia hugged Angie and kissed her good bye.

"We will phone you when we get there, and Angie can speak to you then. We will take good care of her." said Lisa,

"Thanks, she's never been away from me before, I just hope she is ok" said Julia. her voice quivered slightly.

Angie was strapped in next to Tess, the two little girls chatted away lost in their own little world.

"She will be fine, so we will see you on Monday afternoon, around 3ish ok?"

"Fine, see you then, bye bye sweetheart" Julia called to her. She looked up and waved and blew Julia a kiss as the car moved down the driveway. Julia stood at the door and waved till they were out of sight, and wiped a tear from her cheek.

Julia spent the day cleaning and keeping busy. She washed everything that needed or didn't need washing, she dusted and polished furniture swept and vacuumed all through the house, upstairs and downstairs. Ben arrived about four that afternoon to keep her company, something she desperately needed.

Chapter Twenty

The phone rang three times before Mr. Collins answered, "Hello, Collins' residence."

"Mr. Collins, this is Captain Cosgrove, I wonder if I could speak with Ben on an urgent matter."

"He isn't here right now Captain, could I give him a message to call you?"

"I would appreciate it if you could ask him to meet me at the base, as soon as possible, it is rather urgent that he get here, do you think you could do that sir?"

"Yes, Captain, I will do that right away."

"It's for you," said Julia handing Ben the phone.

"Yes I understand, thanks for letting me know dad."

"Look, I have been called back to the base, I had been waiting for this, but I didn't think it would be so soon. I can't really talk about it, you understand, don't you." said Ben.

"Well, just be careful, it is starting to snow again and the roads can be dangerous."

"I know, and I am not looking forward to driving for two hours in it."

Julia kissed him goodbye and he promised to call her when he arrived.

"Make sure you lock up after I leave, I don't like leaving you on your own."

"I'll be fine, now go…the sooner you get this over with the sooner you can be back here with me." He kissed her again, and then he looked into her eyes and said. "I love you Julia, more than I even thought possible"

Julia watched him drive away, and wiped a tear away for the second time that

day.

Chapter Twenty One

He waited till she was inside then crossed the road. The light was fading, he was able to slip inside the gates and move behind the bushes in the garden, he moved silently down the side of the house to the old disused coal shaft, and removed the cover. He let down the rope he had hidden fastened to a tree close to the house, it reached all the way down the shaft. He climbed in and eased himself down the rope to the basement below, as he had done before.

Julia turned off the bath, she stepped into the warm scented water and let it cover her up to her neck, took a mouth full of wine and relaxed. Closing her eyes she thought of Ben, and Angie, they had not rung as yet, she hoped they wouldn't forget. She lay in the bath and just enjoyed the peace. Not long after she heard the phone ringing, dam, she wished she had thought to bring it into the bathroom. She wrapped herself in a towel and ran down the stairs and answered it.

"Hello mummy, we are here and we are having such a good time, Tess' mum and dad got us fish and chips for lunch and they were really yummy, I miss you mummy, but I am being a good girl and using my manners like you said!"

"That's wonderful darling, I'm glad you're having a good time" said Julia, with a small lump in her throat.

She spoke to Lisa and felt better about letting Angie go after all.

Julia went back upstairs, the water in the bath was almost cold, she pulled the plug and put on her warm pajamas and socks. As she sat on her bed about to brush her hair, she heard a noise, it sounded like that noisy bottom step, she sat still and listened, she heard it again. The creak of the bottom step, quietly she went to her bedroom door and peaked over the staircase railing. There in the dull light of the fireplace she could see a figure slowly creeping up the stairs she knew it wasn't Ben.

Terror and panic gripped her. Scared, she looked around her room, she ran to her walk in closet and climbed in behind the long coats she had hanging at the end, she leaned back hard against the wall, she heard a strange "Click" and the wall gave way behind her, she fell backwards onto a cold hard floor she realized she was in some sort of passage way. She stood up and pushed the secret door closed. It was completely black, she couldn't see a thing; no light was coming in from anywhere. She leaned against the door and listened, she could hear him calling her name, he opened the closet door and turned on the light!

Quietly she stepped back, she could feel the cold wall behind her, the damp had soaked her socks and her feet were freezing, but her heart was pounding so hard, she thought he would hear it and find her. She could see a thin line of light under the secret door. He was calling her, by name, she listened to him, who was he, how did he know her, and what did he want!

Chapter Twenty Two

The snow was getting worse; he knew it would take him more than two hours to reach the base. He checked the gauge, petrol was getting low, he looked for a garage so he could fill up and get something hot to eat and drink. After a few more miles he stopped at an all night garage and did just that. He spoke to the attendant about the weather, the attendant told him that a storm was coming in from the north and that he had better keep going on to the base before it hit.

He set off again, it was only another 12 miles, but the snow was falling heavier. He had been expecting to return to the base for more meetings, he just didn't think it would have been so soon. He drove on, the windscreen wipers working hard to keep scraping the snow off the windscreen. The wind seemed to be picking up and the snow getting worse on the slippery roads. He was glad he had fitted the snow chains to the tires before he left the garage as they were now doing their job very well. He could see the light in the base guard box at the entrance. He pulled up and the guard opened the small window.

"Good evening Sir, are you expected?" the guard asked puzzled.

"Well I didn't drive all this way in this weather not to be expected"

"Very good Sir, good night." he replied.

He pushed the button and the automatic arm went up, Ben drove in and headed towards the barracks.

He was looking forward to a hot shower and a warm bed. He knew it was too late to meet with Captain Cosgrove tonight, so he would leave it to the morning.

"Ben? What brings you back here on a night like this?" asked Steve Morton.

"Orders from Cosgrove, I will probably be meeting with him in the morning."

"Are you sure your meeting Cosgrove?" asked Steve.

"My father took a call from him today, said I had to be back here a.s.a.p. why?"

"Well for a start, Cosgrove went to Italy with his wife, he isn't expected back here for at least two more weeks."

"What? are you sure." said Ben

"Positive, he has been looking forward to this holiday for weeks, he only left 3 days ago, we haven't heard anything from him, besides he's on a cruise ship as from yesterday!" said Steve.

"But he rang, my father said it was Captain Cosgrove, I think I'll ring dad there must be some mistake."

After the phone call, he was more confused than ever.

"Dad swears Cosgrove told him that I had to return to the base today. Something is just not right Steve, why did someone want me back here at the base?"

Chapter Twenty Three

Julie stood in the darkened passage; he was calling her, telling her that she and Angie were his family and that he had waited long enough.

She tried to concentrate, to recognize his voice; he sounded like Joe, the wardsman at the hospital where Sally worked. He would always come and speak to Julia and Angie when they came to pick up Sally. He often remarked that Julia should get married so she and Angie would have a real family.

She wondered if it was him. Sally had also told her that he was a very possessive man and a bit strange. But Julia had always found him polite and he always gave Angie some sweets while they waited.

But why was he doing this! Did he once know Robbie, did he know about them? She could hardly think as it was extremely cold in the dark passage way, her feet were almost numb with the cold and she was shivering.

She listened at the door, his voice seemed to be fading away. She carefully pushed at the door and it popped open, she could hear him, the sounds seemed to be coming from down the hall near Sally's room. It sounded like he was opening and closing doors and calling for her to come out.

Julia closed the secret door and stood there alone in the darkness. He had come back into her room shouting for her. After a short time she heard him leave her room again, she popped the door again and listened, she heard the sound she had been waiting for, the creaking of the top and bottom step, she knew he had gone back down stairs.

She opened the door and stepped out into the closet, she took off her wet socks and slipped on some jeans and a thick wool jumper, she took a pair of thick socks from the clothes hamper and put them on to warm her feet with her joggers. She knew she had to get a torch but it was in Sally's room down the hall. She crawled on all fours from her bedroom, he was still downstairs in the kitchen as she could hear him moving around. She kept as close to the walls as possible crawling down to Sally's bedroom. She slowly opened the bedside table drawer and felt around for the torch. She knocked the edge of the drawer and the lamp started to rock! She grabbed it with her other hand before it fell. Her heart pounded, she could feel her body shaking, the tears stinging her fearful eyes. She tucked the torch into her jeans and crawled back to her room. Julia was only a few feet from her bedroom when she heard the sound of the bottom step creaking. She hurried into the room and ran into the closet and climbed back through the secret door, making sure the coats were still in the same position and not exposing the door to the passage way.

Inside she moved to her left away from the door. He was calling to her again.

"Come out Julia, you are mine, I have been patient, I have waited for you for a very long time, you know that, don't you, Angie and you belong to me, we are a family. Come out Julia, come out!"

He was getting very irritated his voice was becoming louder, he was shouting, he sounded angry and dangerous. But his voice, was it Joe?

Fear gripped her if he found the secret door would he kill her, would he harm her in anyway?

Chapter Twenty Four

Julia switched on the torch, she followed the beam down the damp cold passage she rounded a corner and continued along, she came to another secret door and listened, all was quite, she popped it open, it was in Angie's closet, she closed the door and kept on going, she almost slipped as the floor seemed to disappear, shining the torch down she could see a steep stairway, she held onto the rough cold wall and carefully took one step at a time as she climbed down the damp stone steps. At the bottom she shone the torch in front, a few feet away was a wall, a dead end. She looked around to see if another passage lead anywhere, but it was just a blank wall. She heard a noise and quickly turned off the torch. She stood in the darkness, her ears straining to hear any sound. She opened her eyes and blinked to try and adjust to the blackness. It was then that she noticed a small tiny round light, reflecting off the wall opposite. She waved her hand in font of it. Where was it coming from, then she noticed a small peep hole! Quietly she moved towards the hole, closing one eye she looked through it, then something moved and caught her eye. He was walking down the hall towards her like he knew she was there! Julia jumped back against the wall she covered her mouth to stifle a sob. Did he hear her, could he see her!

Shaking uncontrollably she slid down the wall to the ground. She stood up and looked through the peep hole again, she could see him walking up the stairs he was wearing a dark hooded jacket pulled over his head. She tried to picture Joe, his height and build, she wasn't sure that it was him, he looked to thin.

Julia stood in the dark, she had to plan something if she could get to the phone she could call for help. Surely if Ben phoned and she didn't answer, he would come home, but what if he couldn't, she would be left alone with this madman ! She knew she had to get to the phone or to a door but the doors were locked! Keys! Where are the keys..!! She had to take a deep breath so she could think straight. They were in the pants she was wearing, after Ben left she locked the door dropped them in her pocket and went upstairs to her bathroom. She would have to go back and get them. The torch beam was getting dimmer, she shook it and it became a little brighter, but the batteries were fading, she turned it off and tucked it into the jeans, in the darkness she felt her way along the passage to the steps, and climbed them carefully, one by one.

Turning the torch on only when she needed to she found the secret door back to her room, carefully and quietly she opened the door, and crawled out, she couldn't hear anything, where was he? She crept out her closet door and hurried into her bathroom, she found her pants and went through the pockets but the keys were gone! He must have them, she was trapped!

Back in the passage, she remembered that there was a spare key to the conservatorium in the kitchen draw. If she could just get to the phone she may have another chance. Shining the torch in the opposite direction she followed the beam of dim light down the passage, to another flight of steep steps leading down, going towards the back of the house and the conservatorium!

Chapter Twenty Five

At the bottom of the steps was another secret door, popping it open she shone the torch beam into the darkness. It was the storage cupboard under the staircase. It was full of old tennis rackets, skis', suitcases, boxes of books and baby stuff of Angie's. Julia stepped into the cupboard careful not to knock anything over or make any noise as she wasn't sure where in the house he was. The phone was on the hall stand next to the cupboard, she could just reach out and get it.

"RRiingg….rriinngg…" the phone rang loudly.

He came running down the stairs cursing, Julia stood as still as possible she was only on the other side of the door from a madman!

He ripped the phone from the wall and threw it against the cupboard door. He was screaming and cursing. Julia knew he could open the cupboard at any moment and find her there, she quickly and quietly stepped inside the passage and closed the door. She was so afraid she sat on the ground and sobbed.

There was only one other way out, she had to get that key. Back under the staircase cupboard Julia felt him thumping his way back upstairs, telling her no-one could reach her now, he was the only one she would ever need.

She waited by the cupboard door, it took all her courage to open it and step out into the hall, and darted across in to the kitchen, she ran over to the drawer and gently opened it. The door to the conservatory was locked, she hoped that maybe it wasn't. She could hear him coming down the stairs, looking around she spotted the door to the basement and ran over and went inside. She had not been down in the basement in a long time, edging her way down the stairs she hid under the steps in the darkness in case he looked down there. Remembering the last time she came down here with Sally, was to replace a fuse that threw the house into darkness. The fuse box was on the other side of the steps. He was walking around she could follow him above her from the basement, he had gone into the parlor, she heard him, the clink of the glass as he poured himself a drink from Sally's twelve year old scotch!

Shining the torch around she saw old boxes that belonged to Sally's parents and other boxes that contained old books. She piled them on top of each other next to the fuse box. She could feel a cold draft coming from an opening she went over and found the open disused coal shaft with a rope hanging down, and realized that was how he was entering the house.

She tried to climb up the rope but it made too much noise and she knew he would find her. The only chance she had was to take out the fuse and plunge the house into darkness and when he came down to fix it she would push the boxes onto him and escape up to the kitchen, get the key and get out the back door. She couldn't remember if the basement door had a lock on the other side, but it was a chance she had to take! The key was in the second drawer all she needed was a few minutes.

Opening the fuse box, she removed the fuse and hid back behind the boxes. He cursed, the only light was coming from the fireplace, he felt his way along the hall into the kitchen and to the basement door. Standing at the top of the steps he flicked on is cigarette lighter to see into the dark basement and started walking down the steps.

Chapter Twenty Six

Julia moved back into the shadows. He walked over and opened the fuse box, he was using the lighter to find the fuse that Julia had removed, she edged towards the boxes silently and pushed them onto him, he fell to the ground and the boxes were piled on top of him. He screamed at her.

"Come back, you bitch!"

Julia raced up the stairs and slammed the door shut pushed the bolt across and locked the door. She ran to the draw and searched for the key holding the torch in her mouth so she could use both hands. He was banging and hammering on the basement door like a madman. She knew she had to get out, he busted through the door onto the kitchen floor. She ran down the hall, but he was close behind her.

Just as she got to the parlor doorway, he grabbed her from behind and threw her to the floor.

"I told you that I was the only one, why are you fighting me, you belong to me"!

Julia punched and pushed him away from her, but his grip on her arms were too strong, she couldn't get away she could feel his fingers digging into her flesh.

"Who are you, why are you doing this, I don't belong to you, or anyone else, let me go!" she screamed.

Then she saw it, the blade of the knife, glinting in the glow from the fire.

"Oh my God no!" she cried terrified.

He was kneeing over her with the knife pointed at her.

"If I can't have you, then no-one can have you" he screamed in her face.

Just then, the front door burst open someone came flying in and knocked him from her, she rolled over and crouched into a ball, sobbing and shaking. Torch lights were all around her, she could hear voices, they seemed so far away, but they were right beside her.

"Julia, Julia, are you alright?" It was Sally's voice.

She took the fuse from her pocket and handed it to Sally,

"Gilbert, the fuse box, in the basement," she said handing it to him.

The lights came on Julia could see two policemen and Ben, holding down the madman. Ben had knocked him out cold with one punch.

The policeman rolled him over and said, "Do you know this man miss?"

Ben pulled the hood from his head

"Oh my God," said Julia, she fainted.

She woke up on the sofa. Sally was beside her holding her hand.

"Are you alright darling, don't worry, we are here and so is Ben" she said soothingly.

"Do you know who that man is?" said Ben.

"I, I think its Robbie"

"But Robbie is dead" said Sally quietly.

"I know, but."

She was confused and unable to think straight.

"The police want you to make a statement, I told them we would go down to the station and speak to them in the morning." said Ben

Sally poured everyone a scotch and then Ben took her upstairs to bed. He stayed with her the night and promised her would never leave her again.

Chapter Twenty Seven

The next morning they went to the police station, Julia was shown a picture of the man who attacked her. She could barely bring herself to look at it. But when she did, she realized it wasn't Robbie, but James, his brother! He had dyed his hair blonde like Robbie's, James had dark hair before, but he was trying to look like Robbie. Why!

She asked if she could speak with James, Ben was against it at first, but it was something she had to do.

The police constable took her down to the interview rooms. Two policemen stood behind her, James was handcuffed to a steel table.

Julia sat down opposite him, she didn't know what to say to him so she just asked.

"Why James, why did you say I was your family now."

"Because Robbie told me, he said you and Angie were my family now, and I have always loved you and Robbie knew it!"

"But Robbie didn't know about Angie"

"He knew, that girl at the doctor's surgery, she told us about you, being pregnant and not married."

"Robbie knew the baby was his, he told me, then he had the accident, he told me that you both belonged to me now, that I was to be the father and the husband, he knew he was dying, so I promised him, and I knew that you would love me just like you did Robbie!" his voice starting to rise.

Julia sat back in the chair she had been sitting on the edge.

She looked at James and felt so much sorrow for him, now that she was starting to understand. In his mind he thought he could just take over where Robbie left off. He had always loved Julia, and he thought she would love him.

With Robbie gone, it was clear he was to take over and be a father to their unborn child and marry Julia. But when it all went wrong and he had to marry a pregnant Rosina, in his mind coupled with Robbie's death and the death of his own son, he just couldn't cope. It seems he just believed what he wanted in his mind to be the only way. He tracked Julia down and had started watching the house. He started sending things to her and breaking into the house through the old coal shaft and leaving things of Robbie's so she would never forget. It was clear to Julia that James would not be able to stand trial. She felt it would be a very long time before he was sane enough. The Sergeant spoke to Julia when she left James. He too felt that James was in need of psychiatric care.

He promised Julia that he would let her know what would happen to him. Julia dropped all the charges against him. She left the station after making a statement, and knew he would get the help he needed.

They were silent on the drive home, she was trying to understand what had just happened. Ben left her to her thoughts.

Chapter Twenty Eight

Back at home she explained everything to Sally and Gilbert.

"God, you were so brave, I don't think I could have hidden from him like you did!" said Sally

"Oh my God Sally, you don't know do you? Come on I will show you something"

Upstairs Julia took Sally into her closet.

"Remember, when you told me, that your dad said something about secrets in the walls."

"Yes, but he was pretty out of it on morphine, poor love".

Julia pushed back her coats and pushed on the secret door.

'Click' the door opened.

Sally stood with her mouth open and her eyes wide. She looked at the door, then at Julia, then back to the door.

"What the, where does it go, what's behind the door" she asked, astounded at what she was looking at.

"It's a secret door, it leads to passages that surround the house, your father was right, there were secrets in the walls, and that's how I kept away from him, he couldn't find me in the walls."

Julia stood back as Gill and Ben shone torches into the passage still amazed at what they were looking into.

"All I can say is, thank god your dad made these passageways, or I don't know what I would have done. I think they saved my life" said Julia.

"Amen to that" said Ben.

Marianne Conlon

Marianne Conlon is a Sydney writer who writes in an almost hypnotic style. Her contribution to *The Rorschach Montage*, '*Pete And Mary*' seems on the surface very matter of fact almost report like and devoid of emotion. Yet it soon reveals itself to be all about emotions and a very personal essay about love and caring.

Peter And Mary

At first glance the stylish man walking down York street at 7am in the busy city of Sydney looked no different from every one else heading off to work. He was not the most expensively dressed man, but he did look like executive material in his Armin dark blue tailored suit, with crisp white shirt, black and grey striped tie and black polished shoes. The difference about this man, that no one noticed, was that his life was very slowly and utterly shifting off centre, even he did not notice it at first.

Peter Jay started his life on 14th December 1961. He entered this world in a slow and unhurried manner keeping everyone waiting till he was ready. Peter's mother Pam and father John were overjoyed at their son's arrival and were relieved to have such a happy and health son. Two years later Peter's mother had twin girls Emma and Liz, Peter's life shifted a little off centre, he was no longer the one and only, he now had to share with two other crying children that demanded his parent's time. It took awhile for Emma and Liz to endear themselves into Peter's heart, but as time went by Peter learnt how to share his time with both his parents and the girls. Peter's childhood was spent growing up in the southern outskirts of Sydney, the suburb of Sutherland, or as the local's like to refer it as, living in the shire. His neighbourhood appeared average on the surface, but it was made up of some very interesting families and individuals. The neighbours on the right side of Peter's house were Mr and Mrs Kent, they were both Dentists and they had three children. Peter and the girls loved going over to play with the Kent children, it seemed to Peter that they had every new toy that came out on the market. They were very generous and didn't mind if Peter and the girls played with their toys. On the other side live an old couple, Mr and Mrs Jones. Peter would have guessed their age to be as old as 40 years. But for old people they were fun to hang out with, the Jones had no Children and loved having all the kids over in the summer. They had a pool that was far too big for just the two of them.

Peter's band of friends that he had grown up with were Terry, Michael, Mary and his best friend David. The boys could be a bit rough at times but Mary could give as good as she got, she also brought out the softer side of the boys at times. They did everything together, their personalities complimented each other. Peter was the leader, Terry the planner and put together all their adventures. Michael, the voice of reason and caution and Mary the one who grounded them all steering them away from risky escapades. They all loved going to the beach, surfing, playing cricket in the summer and football in the winter. On the weekends Pam, Peter's mum chauffeured them to the usual sporting matches, they even tagged along when Emma and Liz played their netball games and were the girls loudest cheer squad. For Peter's little band life was full of excitement and adventure, not always what they expected but never dull. As they all moved into their teenaged years, Peter's band of friends started to go in different directions. David and Mary went to the same high school as Peter, but Terry had moved house with his family and Michael's parents had sent him to a catholic school.

High school for Peter was difficult at first, having to set your place in the social scheme of the teenage world was not as easy as it looked. Peter shuffled himself down the social ladder instead of up, he did not want to be in the most popular group, that just seemed too much hard work He also didn't want to be too far down either. So he set his sights for the middle, the kids who were just cool enough to avoid being any threat to the who's who group and at no risk of being social outcasts. Mary and David followed Peter on the social scale and life moved along. Learning was easy for Peter, he was one of the lucky ones, he put very little effort into his studies but always came out with a great results. Peter did not have to work too hard in the romance department, either. He was not what you would call handsome, but he did have charm and a smile that a young lady could not resist. Peter's last year at school was complicated. His grades were still impressive, he had left behind a string of broken hearts, voted one of the most promising students in the eyes of his teachers, the most likely to succeed at what ever career he chose. But Peter felt his life was off balance. It took him until the middle of the year to finally figure out what was missing. He was sitting one Monday morning in the library with David, they had some homework to catch up with, when Peter looked up and saw Mary coming in through the library doors. He sat and stared at her for the longest time. It was as if Peter was seeing her for the first time, her eyes meet his and she smiled. In that moment he new that she would be the women he would marry. He marveled at how for all these years, she had walked beside him, been his most trusted friend, he had laughed and cried with her but there was something in the way she looked at him, that same understanding that their friendship have shifted in a new direction.

Peter and Mary entered The University of Sydney. Peter had his heart set on becoming a lawyer, while Mary had always wanted to become a teacher. This was the beginning of their careers. Taking part time jobs, Peter worked at a small cardboard factory until he started his internship with Banks Associates. Mary worked part time in a Gymea Bay nursing home until she started at her first teaching appointment at St Patrick's Primary School. At times their life was not all roses and pink carnation's, there was always bill's to pay, food to put on the table and of course the rent. Even at the end of the week when they only had enough money to get them through to the next pay week, they never doubted that they would not fulfill their dreams.

Peter and Mary were married on the 25th October 1991 at St Mary's Catholic Church Sutherland. It was a grand affair, everyone drank too much and sang too loud but all went home happy. Peter had stayed with Banks after his internship, as he had become one of the firms most promising young lawyers. Mary remained at St Patrick's. Peter and Mary had their first child in 1995, they named him Scott. Then in 1997 they had a daughter who they called Emma. Pete's family circle was complete, his life was travelling along with the usual twists and turns, surprises and disappointments that life has a tendency to throw at you, but nothing that shook their little world too much. Peter at times, at the end of a long day, would sit with a cold Tooheys beer and marvel at how lucky he and his family were. He would reminisce about his life, he knew how he had been blessed and that other's were not as fortunate. He only allowed himself to ponder on occasion as he did not want to tempt fate and draw attention to himself and his fortunate life.

Mary's and Peter's life moved along with all the usual little dramas. Their working careers thrived. Mary became deputy principle after returning to work when the children started school. Peter was made a partner in his law firm. Life was filled with work and on weekends running around with the children. Like Peter, Scott and Emma enjoyed all the benefits that living in the Shire provided. They belonged to Cronulla Surf Club nippers, Emma played netball and tennis, Scott loved playing football and cricket. Peter and Mary shared the chauffeuring, which they did not mind as they loved being so involved in their children's lives.

Peter's life started to shift ever so slightly after his fiftieth birthday. He could not put his finger on it, but he started becoming aware that something was not right. At first he put his forgetfulness down to working too hard and running around with the kids. It was just little things at first, like misplacing his keys, forgetting to pick up milk and bread after work. Mary would tell him how her day was and by after tea he was unable to recollect what she had said. Nobody took any notice at first as they just excepted that he was just over doing it. But cracks started to show at work, Peter had difficulty with putting together briefs for new cases, he would ask his secretary the same question a few times before he had realised he had already asked her. He was getting home later and later. Mary started to worry, she tried to speak to him but he just became angry and distant. Scott and Emma also started to notice a change in their father, he would make up excuses so he was unable to take them to their sporting events on the weekend. He was quick to anger and refused to ask them any questions in case he had already asked them and had forgotten. He was spending more time in the study isolating himself from his family using the excuse that he had some very big cases coming up at work. Six months had gone by when one night he was heading home and he found himself driving over the Iron Cove Bridge, going in the complete opposite direction from his home. Peter started to panic, he had no idea were he was or how to get home, he pulled off the main road into a side street, parked the car and turned off the engine. What to do next he had no idea, he was unable to collect his thought's they were like a world wind inside his head, he could feel them swimming around but he was unable to crab a single thought.

It started to get dark, Mary was starting to be worried when she came home at 8 o'clock and Peter was not home. She had spoken to him earlier during the day and he said he would be home by 7 o'clock. She checked her phone, there were no messages or miscalls. Mary rang his phone, on the last ring he answered. Mary had to ask if she had the right number as the person on the other end did not sound like her husband. Mary was not able to understand at first what the man was saying, he sounded anxious and confused, it took a few minutes before she was able to gently calm the man down. She finally realised that she had been speaking with her husband all along. She had a sinking feeling that something terribly wrong was happening to her husband. After half an hour of encouraging Peter to describe his surroundings, Mary had a rough idea were he was. She told him to stay put and she would be there soon, which she realised after hanging up was a wasted statement as Peter was incapable of moving anywhere. Mary rang Peter's mother Pam and quickly explained the situation, she would be right over to pick her up.

On the way Mary told Pam all the strange things that had been happening to Peter, all the forgetfulness, the sudden outbursts out anger when Mary tried to talk to him, him asking the same questions over and over. Spending more time in his study, isolating himself from her and the children. Pam sat and listened, with each strange behaviour Mary spoke about she became more and more sure that Mary was talking about someone who was exhibiting behaviours associated with dementia. This could not be possible as this was an old people's decease. Pam did not share her concerns with Mary, but she could not shake her feeling of despair.

They finally found Peter, he was sitting in his car in the dark. Mary got out of the car and rushed over to him, he turned his head and looked at her. There was no recognition in his eyes at first as to who she was, she spoke his name and he looked at her again, this time he recognised her and started to cry uncontrollably. Mary held him until his tears were spent. He looked into his wife's eye's and asked her what was happening to him, Mary said to him she did not know but they would find out. Mary drove Peter's car and Pam followed them home. Mary ran a bath for Peter when they got inside, he was not hungry and went straight to bed. Mary asked Pam to stay the night, Pam poured both of them a straight shot of scotch. They sat in the back lounge, discussing the night's events and all the strange things that had been happening over the last six months. Three hours later, it was decided that Mary and Peter were to go to their Doctor in the morning. Both Mary and Pam had heard the word dementia and all the strange behaviours that Peter was presenting, were associated with this disease. Mary argued that everything she had heard about dementia was that it was an old people's problem. Pam knew a little more about it as she was older and had a friend's husband who was diagnosed, but he was in his seventies. Both women had very little sleep that night. Peter was the only one who slept well. In the morning realisation crept into Peter's mind, that after last night's event's he could no longer deny that something very strange was happening to him. Mary talked to him over breakfast, she told him how worried she and his mother were. He agreed to go to the doctor with her.

Sitting in the Doctors office Peter was having difficulty breathing and his concentration was failing. He started to take big breaths and just focus on slowing his breathing down. He could hear Mary talking as if she were far away and he just could not quite hear or understand what she was saying. It seemed a long time before his conscious self appeared in the room with Mary and the doctor. His eyes started to re-focus and when they cleared he sat staring at Mary and the doctor who had stopped talking and were watching him. The doctor realised that Peter, although in the room physically, had not been there mentally. So very slowly and in a very quite but reassuring way he asked Peter to describe all the odd things and feelings he had been experiencing over the last few months. At first Peter just stared at the doctor, then as the doctor's words came drifting into his consciousness ever so slowly, he started to talk. At first there were just single words he used to describe how he was feeling.

Words like lost, confused, scared, angry, frustrated, inadequate, stupid, liar. Then he started to use sentences to describe the emotions he had been experiencing. Trying to gather his thoughts, not like the way the terminology is used in novels but literally trying to grab each thought and placing it in a sentence that he recognised or understood. If you could imagine sitting and having all these words that you have used all your life just spinning around in your head and you have lost the way to put the puzzle together. He was not experiencing this all the time, but he did admit that it was happening more often. The doctor told them that he wanted to take some blood to see if there was anything physical that could be causing this change in him. He also wanted Peter to do a written test which assessed a person's cognitive functions. He gave Peter a referral to have a CAT scan on his brain to see if there were any changes occurring. There are a number of diseases that can causes dementia, it would take time and be a process of elimination. Peter and Mary left the doctor's office in a daze, neither one was sure how they had gotten home, Mary must have drove as they were sitting in their driveway. They sat there for an hour, both turned and looked at each other. Mary spoke to her husband, saying it did not matter what the outcome of all these tests, he was her husband and the love of her life and no matter how their life shifted off centre that would never change. Peter held his wife and they both cried at the way their life was going to change and all the challenges they would encounter in the future. They stayed in their car until the kids came out looking for them, then Mary and Peter got out of the car and walked into their home with the children.

Peter and Mary never cried again about how life had thrown them a life changing blow, they just shifted and adjusted their life with each new challenge.

Jorge Zeledon

Jorge Zeledon is an Australian citizen, originally from Nicaragua, a country in Central America. Twenty-four years ago he arrived in Australia as a refugee under the United Nations refugee resettlement program to Australia. He was a university student in the 1980's when civil unrest took place in his homeland followed by a nine year long cruel and bloody civil war which tore apart his country and family. He managed to escape to Honduras in a brave and risky adventure. Taken as a prisoner by the Honduran army, jailed and tortured, he then spent two years in a refugee camp surviving harsh and difficult conditions one can only imagine. Successfully, he applied to migrate to Australia. Once in Australia, he completed his tertiary studies in Horticulture Science and Landscaping and integrated himself into the Australian society. Married to Ruth and the proud father of Byron and Lachlan, he is currently living in Western Sydney. He believes that sharing his story will encourage young people to achieve their goals and thrive, despite the hurdles life may bring upon them and make a contribution for a great country which is Australia.

Hola Zorro

Sometimes we say life is a journey but it is more than that. Life is a school of never ending experiences. Some of them planned and others come across our lives without any possible control over them. For example, our biological development, the effect of natural disasters, accidents, diseases, political prosecution or a civil war.

I would like to share my personal story, perhaps a journey full of events that shaped my personal life in many ways as I became a survivor of a civil war that tore apart my family and my country during the 1980's. It is my intention throughout this story to remain politically neutral and adhere to a narrative chain of events, a testimonial exercise, and a flow of events truly and factually as they happened back then, where it happened and how it happened.

The whole story began in Nicaragua during the nine year long civil war between the Contra rebels and the Sandinista government in charge since 1979, after a political revolution, all this within the context of the east and west conflict in the international political arena, better known as the Cold War.

Nicaragua is geographically in the middle of Central America sharing common borders with Honduras to the north and Costa Rica to the south, an exuberant tropical country of rivers, volcanoes, lakes and mountains with diverse flora and fauna and a very touristic country indeed. The Pacific area is the most densely populated and here is where the capital of Managua is located. The other areas are, the Central Mountains, the Atlantic area with the entire population being seven million people.

I was born in the central mountains region of Nicaragua where agriculture and cattle grazing are the main activities, the second son of an extended family of ten. Back then my father owned a couple of cattle ranches and my mother was a primary school teacher. She provided home schooling for us organising a small primary school in one of the ranches. She always supported and encouraged us to excel in education as a means of progress and achieving new horizons. As we grew older my parents decided to move into a small town nearby, called Matiguas, where we could continue our formal education and this worked out very well for all of us.

It was a known fact that during the 1960's and 1970's there were a lot of new political movements emerging in the South American countries and Central America was affected by such political turmoil. A political revolution led by the historic Sandinista movement overthrew the existing government in 1979, this being the beginning of a new social and political era for Nicaragua and the starting point for new challenges, changes for me as a teenager hungry to succeed in life.

Due to the new government policies, there was a national reaction of the people of Nicaragua; the same people who historically helped them out to victory months ago. As a result of this situation, a civil war commences. It was a violent and cruel war costing more than 50,000 people dead and extremely devastating for the national economy. At this stage in my life, all of my brothers and sisters were studying either at the national university, high school or primary school.

The setting of this war was mostly in the mountains of central Nicaragua and the border line to the north with Honduras and in the Pacific area where the major cities are. Life was going on apparently as "normal", business activities, schools and universities open but the population felt the impact of the war as the shortages of food and supplies became more and more evident. The whole country was in a struggle. The government declared a national emergency and compulsory military service was introduced as well. This was 1983, a turning point for thousands of families in Nicaragua. A massive exodus to Honduras, Mexico, Costa Rica and El Salvador began and refugee camps emerged in these neighbouring countries.

The five eldest siblings from our family, three boys including myself and the two eldest girls, were all studying at the National

University. Every year we were forced to work in the cotton fields in the Pacific areas or the coffee bean plantations in the north or central mountains. This was when our exodus began, the younger of my sisters who was at university fled to Mexico as a refugee, she was the first. We boys decided to stay but this did not work out too well.

My younger brother that followed me, and I, were conscripted by the national army and requested to go out to the battle fields after three months of infantry training. We managed to escape before arriving at the training bases and lived in hiding in the capital city of Managua. This hiding period was very dangerous because the secret police kept every single house under strict surveillance. Sometimes we needed to hide inside the ceiling cavity, eat there and late at night come down to sleep. At this point in time the civil war was escalating to new heights; the whole country was at war.

My parents started preparing a way to escape from Managua to either Honduras or Costa Rica. Males between sixteen and forty years old had their passports confiscated so going across the mountains was the only choice. I was willing to take the risk and go.

Nicaragua, as a tropical country, has only two weather seasons, a long rainy winter which is from May to November and a dry summer with occasional storms for the rest of the year. I decided to go north across the border line and reach Honduras, aiming to get to the refugee camps already established there.

My uncle provided his ute as transport and I dressed as a peasant in typical working clothes and hat. It was a rainy morning in July when we left for our trip, but previous to this day a lot of homework had to be done regarding planning the trip and different scenarios to consider, in a way it seemed like an adventure was beginning. For example, distances of travel, army check points on the way, places to stay, the towns near the border, answers for the possibility of being questioned at any check point, degree of danger, the consequences if we were caught, jail term and even death for avoiding compulsory military service.

When a desire of freedom is present, combined with the willingness to take risks, nothing can stop you from going ahead. I was young, full of dreams and optimism to conquer life. As I had mentioned before, it was winter and at this time had been raining and all week it had been overcast and according to a friend in the family it was ideal to use these conditions as a distracting factor on the trip. It was a very sad goodbye, I still remember the tears running down my mother's face, a hard thing to avoid knowing how brave she was but inside of me was a burning desire to leave the country.

Quickly, I jumped in the back of the ute. In Central America to travel in the ute's rear, known as pick-up trucks, is allowed. Some of them have a wooden cage, a very typical mode of travelling there. The time was 8:00am and we start heading north, a bit nervous but we disguised it with a smile.

As we travelled a good thirty minutes, we were ready to approach the first check point. My uncle, who was driving, slowly stopped and waited for the heavily armed soldier to talk to us and search us as well. Thank God they just waved and signalled us to keep going. We just looked at each other in disbelief but it was true … the soldiers did not stop us. Considering that the intelligence service was always one of the best, we knew that the following check point, at the main cross road called Sebaco, would be a critical one, located right at the central region of Nicaragua, a very strategic position joining main roads to the Atlantic area and the north.

The rain continued as we travelled north, the wind splashed the water on my face due to the speed of the ute, it did not bother me as we were very much aware of the danger that lay ahead in one hour's travel. I knew the area very well as I used to travel through here from my hometown to the capital city. This spot was very popular, a kind of market place where buses from different areas of the country could stop and the passengers relax for fifteen minutes, go for a cold tropical drink or an aromatic cup of home produced and flavoured coffee.

As we approached the area, the rain was heavy and my heart started beating faster, everything felt so tense. Fifty metres ahead was a group of soldiers on duty protected by a small wooden shelter. My uncle slowed down enough to hear any request from the soldiers. For a moment I felt that I wasn't breathing, the rain droplets sounded so hard and heavy. A few seconds seemed like long minutes, not a single voice from the soldiers; they waved us to move on as my uncle drove away slowly. Once again, I survived crossing one of the spots most heavily guarded by the government security service.

In three hours time we needed to get to the small town near the borderline with Honduras, more rain, no time to stop and have some lunch or a drink. Time was so crucial for this adventure. My uncle, the driver, knew that for everyone who did this, ten years jail term was the penalty if we were caught, so it was not easy for him but everyone was happy the way our journey was unfolding hour by hour.

At this time the rain ceased a bit and this worried us but then suddenly it resumed heavier than before. While travelling a lot of thoughts crossed my mind, such as the unknown future in Honduras, my uncle's personal security once he returned from this mission, my family's as well, but freedom has a high price and I was willing to pay for it. As I was deep in my thoughts, we approached the small town which is only one hour away from Honduras. This zone was the scene of combat between the Contras and the Sandinista soldiers fighting far into the mountains. A few army trucks passed us in the opposite direction maybe towards the capital to get more supplies. As we entered this little town a few soldiers were patrolling the area. Nothing happened here, the main action was in the mountains that I expected to cross the next day.

My uncle stopped at this little hotel, he explained to the owner that we would like a room to stay for the night. The trip had been long and tiresome and I really needed to rest. The owner asked, "Are you visiting or going north?" My uncle replied that we had come for the festivities to have fun and drink some wine, the owner believed him.

We had dinner and my uncle left the premises as I went to my room, promising he will be back in the morning. The rain was on and off all night, I could not sleep staying here as a stranger due to the risk involved in my trip and what lay further ahead.

My next step was to catch a small bus to the mountain pass that would issue a visa if you have all your documents in order, a place administered by some customs officers. This place was like a customs service for quick access to Honduras. Obviously this would not help me at all. My plan was to get off the bus long before this point, knowing beforehand that walking north would get me to Honduras in one hour.

Around here everything was dense vegetation and mountain patrols combed this area regularly, as did the Honduran army. So that was the situation, one more step and I would be in another country or in the hands of the Sandinista army, who would be able to sleep with such an adventure and real danger? That night went so slowly, I remember looking at the ceiling all night long and rain droplets sounded like clear small stones falling on the rooftop.

Early in the morning I thanked the hotel owner for his hospitality and started walking to the market place to catch the bus travelling north. I paid my fare and I sat down near the door as few people got into the bus. I was a stranger in the area but also a lot of people travelled this way for small business transactions, this gave me a sense of relief. Half an hour later, I signalled the driver to stop and I walked away on the road until the bus disappeared around a bend, then I entered the bush, beautiful landscape, tall trees, dense shrub, creeks, hills, everywhere clean air with fragrant pine trees. The ground was very soft due to the overnight rains.

I had studied this area before and I was sure that in about twenty or thirty minutes I would be in Honduran territory.

Walking carefully, checking the ground and avoiding any noise from my walking, I walked and walked and walked for about forty minutes but because of the danger itself, it seemed to be longer than an hour. I started to get nervous and then I tripped over a cow carcass and immediately remembered that some areas in the mountains had been planted with landmines. A chill feeling crossed my back, I was in real danger.

I said to myself, I'm sure I've already crossed to Honduras. In central America, like some other countries in the world, the government uses natural landmarks like rivers, volcanoes, mountain ridges to define boundaries and borderlines otherwise they pitch concrete columns of one metre in height along the territory with some geographic information written on it.

As I kept walking, I was feeling more nervous and desperate but I did not have a choice, going back was not an option, I must keep going. Suddenly, I started running then as I reached a small creek I heard a low and clear command, "STOP AND PUT YOUR HANDS UP!" I did not move at all. When I saw who it was I was scared, it was a group of soldiers wearing camouflage uniforms and absolutely very well armed. For a moment I thought, this is the Sandinista army and they will kill me right there! Seeing my expression of fear, one officer stepped ahead and shouted, "Don't be scared, we belong to the Honduran army, we are not going to kill you but you are under arrest for crossing the border illegally." That was a relief! They started interrogating me and they did a body search and for some reason, which until this day I don't know, they suspected that I was a spy from the Sandinista government. So they told me to follow them to their base where they would be investigating me. For a moment I thought, I made it, I am in Honduras, I am alive! For me it was a victory in itself, I didn't care that I was a new prisoner for this army.

After two hours of walking, we arrived at their mountain post. They never came close to me and were always pointing their weapons at me while they communicated by radio. Within an hour an army truck arrived with some soldiers as well. They ordered me to climb onto the back of the truck and they drove back to their main base. Not one of the soldiers said a single word to me and were always pointing their machine guns at me. Once we arrived, they took my name and explained that the investigation procedure will take a few days. I did not care about it at the beginning, inside me a celebration was going on, being here was so important for me. Immediately they took me to the prisoners' cell, this is very interesting stuff. In this cell which was about 20 square metres, there were no beds, prisoners slept on the floor using cardboard as blankets. The toilet was in one corner totally open, they manage to do their business in front of fifteen or more prisoners. A light bulb in the ceiling was lit up day and night. Within days you would not know the difference between day and night.

Nothing about these conditions bothered me, I was alive! In Honduras the prison system does not provide food for inmates, family and relatives must provide food, clothing and other provisions that you may need in jail. Only high security jails supply the basics for prisoners.

This was my second day without food or any kind of shower except the heavy rain two days before which gave me a cold shower indeed. It is amazing how the human body can tolerate lack of food, lack of personal cleansing but never lack of sleep. After a few hours inside this jail I fell asleep for hours, I was extremely tired. I awoke because of the inmates making noise, I did not know what time it was. I started feeling hungry and another prisoner shared his lunch with some of us, at least I had something in my stomach.

Most of the prisoners started asking questions such as; why are you here? Did you kill someone? Where did you come from? etc. We were talking when an officer entered the jail and ordered me to follow him, which I did. Immediately after taking me into another room, he started accusing me of being a spy for the Sandinistas. That is dangerous and I needed to tell him the whole truth about how I got there. I started that I was a university student running away from the war, he felt insulted by my answer and hit me, then put a gun to my head. I was terrified because back in the cell my fellow prisoners had commented about the brutality of this investigation unit. I kept my declaration; he hit me again and then sent me back to the jail cell.

Three days later he came back with another officer, they always wore black glasses, took me to another room and they put me to do physical exercises, push-ups and sit-ups, to the extreme, asking the same questions. They got angry again then one of them took a stick and ordered me to put my hands with my finger tips up, they started hitting my fingertips and within seconds I was bleeding. They waited until the blood stopped and then back to jail. This happened in the very first week. More prisoners share their food with me and when I asked about a shower, they laughed and said, if you're lucky they call us outside and hose us down for a few minutes. Some of them had gone months without a shower.

As I entered into the second week in jail, my morale was still high, maybe because I had crossed the border line, this thought was keeping me alive emotionally. More interrogations, more beatings and back to jail. Sometimes I thought, will they kill me in the middle of the night, at times this worried me.

It was during the third week that two officers called me and took me to a small office. Members of the International Red Cross were visiting the jail looking for Nicaraguan refugees; they told me that by that afternoon I will be transported to the refugee camps with a group from Nicaragua. They let us call our relatives in Nicaragua, I called my aunty. At 3pm a truck arrived and waited for us, I said goodbye to my good friend in jail and I walked towards the truck and got in. A sense of happiness, relief and joy invaded me, at least my personal situation was making some progress and I was leaving this horrible jail.

A few refugees were in the back of this truck, most of them peasants from the north of Nicaragua and a few students as well. We left this town at about 3:30pm on a sunny afternoon. I approached the students, they were from the capital city, Managua. One of them, barely eighteen years old, looked very distressed. He told me that he had been lost for a week eating grass and leaves and drinking water when he was found by the Honduran army. Sharing his story relaxed him a bit.

Our truck was very smelly because it was used to transport cattle but not having had a shower for three weeks, the smells seemed to blend very well. The road was full of pot holes because of the heavy rain in this season but the scenery was fantastic; green hills, big mountains of pine trees, cattle and horses everywhere.

At 5pm the truck entered a dusty town, a small sign on the road greeted us, "Welcome to Teupasenti", an old abandoned town in the Honduran country side with a few shops open and streets full of rocks. As we crossed this town toward the International Red Cross offices, the truck needed to stop a few times due to the herd of donkeys, pigs, hens and ducks walking peacefully on the street, a very interesting sight in this isolated town. Finally, the truck stopped in front of a very well fenced off blue building. The national flag of Honduras was next to the Red Cross flag, undulating in the nice afternoon breeze.

The driver told us to get off the truck and he would guide us to the main office. Once inside they asked our name and relation with the rest of the group then they proceeded to give us some cooking utensils, a plate, a cup, raw groceries like rice, beans, coffee and some soap, a camping mat, a blanket, just the bare necessities to survive in the camp.

The administrator or manager of this office was very polite, his name was Alejandro. Within thirty minutes everyone was ready with food supplies and blankets and the Red Cross personnel seemed to be happy providing us with the basics. Back to the truck and heading off to our new destination, a refugee camp by a big river, called Hortalizas. Within ten minutes we arrived at the camp, fenced off with barbed wire, which was occupied with two thousand refugees. All around soldiers patrolled and hundreds of army canvas tents were set up aligned in rows. The truck stopped in front of a large wooden building that functioned as a school. A big crowd of refugees gathered around asking questions about the war and which part of Nicaragua we were from.

The Red Cross personnel separated us and allocated students with students and peasants with peasants; I did not know anyone there. Once we settled in our tent, we decided to go to the river, how refreshing at last to have a nice bath. Back to the tent, hunger did not bother me as I fell asleep immediately. I really needed a good rest, I must have slept about ten hours.

I awoke and got out of my tent and I felt more relaxed. A few curious people came to talk and then walked away. Some people offered me food, that was very kind of them. It did not take me a long time to figure out the camp conditions as I saw children suffering from malnutrition, a lot of elderly people seriously ill and the state of mind of everyone; sadness to be in a foreign country, refugees as a social status, not allowed to work and with a lot of limitations. Hope to return and go back to our country was the general opinion but the civil war was in its third year with six more years to go, not that we knew when it would end at that time.

Located in a rural area, the camp did not have basic services such as electricity, clean drinking water or a sewerage system. We burned timber to light up our tents and there were fifty out-houses three hundred metres from the camp, which we used as toilets. The river was our main source of water and cleansing as well and firewood as fuel for cooking purposes. There were some strict rules in which everyone must work in certain duties such as, chopping wood, teaching at the school, cleaning or agriculture work.

The town nearby was only twenty minutes away, this was where the camp's administration office was located. Refugees were allowed to visit the office but everyone had to return to the camp in the evening. If any refugee was caught wandering the streets at night, they would be locked up in jail so escaping from this place was not a choice because without documents the authorities would find you anyhow. An international organisation called CARITAS helped out with medical assistance but was very limited in resources and medical supplies.

The administration of the camp faced a serious problem with food supplies from the United Nations. The situation was that every week more and more refugees arrived and the number of registered refugees changed every day. Hunger and frustration showed up, children and elderly people were the most affected, seeing hundreds of people without food is something that gets you emotionally deep inside. As the number of refugees increased to five thousand, the existing problems were getting worse and frustration reigned in the camp. Some people decided to go and join the Contra rebels and fight.

As I mentioned before, the camp's population was mostly peasants and a few hundred students, mostly of university level. Most of us students aimed to go as wetbacks to the United States, not one of us had a passport so heading to North America was a challenging venture. A lot of people tried but they got stopped in the neighbouring countries or by the local security and they put them in jail, releasing them after investigation.

I remembered applying to the Embassy of Canada but they rejected me. I wrote to charity organisations across the United States and I never heard anything back. This time was quite upsetting and affecting me psychologically and my relatives could not visit me because of the risks involved.

My first Christmas in the camp was just another sad night in my tent. Being involved in working activities made the situation more bearable, in a way it worked out as therapy. A year passed, the camp got bigger and a few people left but the conditions were the same. Back in Nicaragua it was another year of fighting and nothing was achieved, nobody achieves anything in a war.

One morning an international delegation from the United Nations was visiting and asking all students to gather because they wanted to talk to us. Well, that was interesting, something different as we were used to visitors being mostly journalists from Europe and the United States. They told us that Australia was willing to resettle some refugees subject to Australia's migration criteria. Some written information was given away and at the end of their information talk it was question time and they asked us to show with our hands up, who were interested in this resettlement program. There were many hands up so they promised to come back the following week.

Once they left, there were a lot of comments as to what Australia was offering, that it was so far away and even a rumour that they needed slaves in the mines and so on. Full of optimism, I filled out my application form and waited for their feedback.

Months passed by and we never heard any news about it, until in the middle of the day a social worker and other people visited our camp with a list of names and invited us to a meeting in a little hall, everyone was happy to be inside at that meeting. The information was straight forward and to the point. We have only thirty applicants from both refugee camps who filled out the applications and everyone will have the chance to be interviewed and whoever qualified to the Australian migration criteria will be offered new settlement. They let us ask questions about Australia and we got a lot of information, they specifically clarified the rumour of "modern slaves" in the mines. As they left, they promised to be back within two months, a positive atmosphere was in the air with the hope that there will be a third country for us.

In the camp, for us it was the same routine, working activities, more refugees arriving, food shortages, diseases etc., a cruel reality that was affecting us all in different ways. First month passed, no news about the anxiously awaited decisive interview. Two weeks later a message came to the administration office, "Please advise the following refugees to be ready on Monday at 7am". What news! Our destiny was unfolding somehow, this day was chosen by the United Nations personnel and the Australian migration officers.

As I mentioned earlier on, our limitations became more evident, food was the main concern but shoes and clothes were scarce as well, how on earth will anyone of us be decently dressed for the interview? Short pants and singlets were the most common way of dressing. I borrowed some clothes and thongs, because going bare foot was really embarrassing for this special occasion.

The truck arrived on time, we were ready. As they read out our names we jumped into this cattle truck, what a moment! We were all so happy. On the way they told us that our destination was Danli, a small city which I knew very well while I was in the jail at the beginning of my adventure. We started joking around saying; the United Nations is taking us to a hotel with food and drinks provided. Well, it was just a good joke because we did not eat at all during the day. As the truck was approaching the city it turned away to the outskirts, where all the cattle farms were located. The truck stopped at one of these ranches or haciendas, they told us to get off and wait outside near a cattle shelter, it surprised us, but at this stage we did not care. As we waited a very well dressed United Nations officer came to us and politely introduced himself and explained that due to budget restraints they could not take us to a more decent place. We laughed about it and told him that this did not matter then he talked about the interviewing procedure; to give them twenty minutes and then they will ready to call us.

The decisive day has come, we were nervous but optimistic. One of us suggested, the first person called must tell us all the questions so we will be one step ahead, so under such a situation no one wanted to be first. The doors opened wide, the distance to the interview panel was about twenty metres, we stayed quiet waiting for the name of the first person to face the music, "Jorge Zeledon" the officer called. I remember it so well. I started walking with a positive attitude and a big smile on my face, what an experience! There were three people in the interview panel, an Australian immigration delegate, a psychologist and a representative from the United Nations. They politely introduced themselves and I mutually did the same.

Each one of us took a turn during the interview process asking and answering questions; "What are you going to do if you go to Australia?" "Work, learn the language and study something at technical or professional level", that is how I answered this question. The rest of the questions were about my academic background in Nicaragua, my family including brothers and sisters, how I came to Honduras, how dangerous was Nicaragua and my personal contribution to help in the camp, it took about thirty minutes. I was always confident and very optimistic. After I finished I thanked them for the opportunity to have an interview. They very clearly stated that being interviewed will not guarantee a resettlement, a commission will assess our interview results and a personal letter will inform of the interview outcome within the next three months.

We thought it was fair, let us wait and hope for the best. As I walked away they called the second candidate, briefly I whispered the questions asked, I wanted to help as we saw each other as brothers at the camp. The second person comes back and we asked what sort of questions they were asked, the questions were a bit similar. Soon we realized that our own personal attitude was highly considered so we could not have the same answers, besides the interview panel was one of good expertise and we were beginners. One by one we were interviewed and by 3:00pm they finished and again politely reminded us to wait for the letter.

Very optimistic, we go back to the truck and start heading back to the camp, we joked around as if we were in Australia, talking some English words, dreaming about it, letting our imagination fly free and enjoy a bit of happiness thinking of being relocated to another country. After two hours we arrived back to our own reality, a few friends asked about the interview and wished us all the best. I had something to eat and I went in to my tent, talked about it with the group of refugees with whom I shared this tent then I fell asleep. What a day it was, I was mentally exhausted.

My duties at the camp were teaching primary children in the morning and adults in the afternoon but my favourite one was going to the mountains in an organised group to fell down trees that later on will be supplied at the camp to be used as fuel for cooking purposes. Staying in mountain camp usually took a week of hard working but was the best therapy for us far away from the camp; away from sick children, depressed people and so much suffering, a temporary relief at least.

Three months passed and we asked every day for any information from the Australian embassy. One afternoon some officers from the Red Cross and the United Nations arrived at the camp and wanted to see us as soon as possible. It did not take long for us to go and meet them, this is something that I will never forget in my life. They said we got some information for you inside these envelopes, as they began to give them away. The ones who got the letters started jumping with happiness thinking that they will go to Australia, all letters were delivered and I did not get one. For a minute I was devastated, sad and angry, how could it be possible. I asked the visitors if there were more letters on the way, the answer was a straight no. Then something interesting happened, one refugee opened his letter and as he was reading his happiness turned away, the letter stated that unfortunately, his intention to be resettled was unsuccessful. Everyone got the same message, what a tragedy, a real sad experience for those who received a letter but then I started thinking maybe the rest of us will be travelling. It was a possibility, just a hope, something to dream about anyway.

Three days passed and by midday there was a request from the Red Cross office, they wanted to see us by 1:00pm. We ran to the office, in no time we were at the doorsteps of this office. Once everyone was there, they invited us inside, an extreme silence fell in the room as one officer spoke, "Congratulations to all of you, Australia is willing to take you as residents." I personally thanked the officer for such good news, we did not know what to do, even with the best news we could not believe it. What a memory, what a day, what an opportunity, our long wait was finally over.

They informed us that the following months will be for medical examinations and then they will advise when the trip will be. As we came back to the camp we shared the news and some of the refugees, they congratulated us and I felt sorry for the rejected ones. It took a few days for this news to sink in my mind.

A message comes across from the administration office, the first group of three needs to go for the medical checkups. Once again, I borrowed some shoes, a shirt and a pair of shorts at least to look a bit presentable. They took us to Danli, that was January 1986 and most of us have the medical done and all come out good. After a few days the first group was ready to travel, I was in this group. We got a letter saying that we will be travelling the 20th of February 1986 to the capital city of Honduras and after that travel to Australia. As everyday passed by I was anxious, nervous, happy but at the same time I sympathised with the rest of the refugees.

Finally, one Tuesday afternoon a four wheel drive car arrived at the camp, a friend gave me an old pair of shoes, another one handed me a shirt and I wore my old cargo shorts. I was ready to go but saying good bye to the refugees staying behind was one of the hardest experiences I have came across. I remember it very well, as I started exchanging handshakes my voice began to disappear and some tears rolled down my face. I could not believe how sad I felt and how difficult this moment was for me, some said to me that hard work had helped us to get out of there.

We left the camp and within minutes we were in town and as we travelled I looked back so many times to this refugee camp and the dusty town to which I arrived two years ago, all was history now. After three hours we entered into Tegucigalpa, the capital city of Honduras and we stopped at this little hotel where all the United Nations employees came for lunch or dinner. A room was enough for us three, I sat in the living room, a small television unit was on and I enjoyed a bit of life style sitting down on the sofa, quite a difference after sitting down on hardwood logs for two years. Soon was dinner time, a complete meal. I ate that meal in minutes followed by a nice tropical refreshment, what a feast, I still remember to this day.

Within two days I had to leave the country, the officers advised us that a special travelling document was issued by the United Nations to assist us with this special situation. I asked the officer if there was any chance to call my relatives back in Nicaragua. They kindly took me to Hondutel, the communications office in this city, and I called my aunty to give the message to my parents. I believed the officers felt sorry about my condition because the next day took me to a clothing store to buy some new and decent clothes and shoes for my trip. Once I had chosen my clothes, they paid for them and we came back to the hotel where a lovely dinner waited for us and a good night's rest. As they left they told us they will be back at 8:00 am the next morning to take us to the airport.

Very early in the morning I was ready, the officers came on time, they gave me a white plastic bag with the United Nations logo printed in blue, and I have kept this special bag with me to this day. Once I arrived at the airport they helped us to check in and gave me 20 US dollars. We waited thirty minutes and finally they called my name to board. I said goodbye and I thanked them for the last time as I walked away to the boarding gate. Mexico was my first destination and we landed within hours. As everybody prepared to exit, an announcement was made for passengers going to Los Angeles. Immediately people needed to board, I kept walking with the other passengers when suddenly two secret police officers took me by each arm and said, "Please come with us, we need to talk with you" and they asked for my passport. I explained that the pilot has my travelling visa, they did not believe me and told me that I was under arrest and facing deportation within forty-eight hours to Nicaragua. I could not believe my luck as they locked me in a small room and off they went to enquire about my situation and what I had told them. Twenty minutes later they come back and apologised, I was angry for such a misunderstanding and that this incident had occurred at this critical stage of my trip.

Once on board, a sense of relief came to me and a few hours later I arrived at Los Angeles airport. I got out and I made sure my documents were handed to the plane crew, which happened as I expected. This was a midnight flight, a very long trip of thirteen hours when we landed at around 10am. I took my plastic bag and joined the queue for customs procedures.

As I waited in line, the other passengers went through with a lot of luggage, a customs officer called me and asked about my luggage so I just showed him my plastic bag and handed my documents. They were impressed as they gave me a nice welcome and wished me good luck. After finishing with customs, two immigration officers informed me that my next destination was the Villawood Migrant Hostel, where hundreds of migrants were housed upon arrival. Today this facility is used as a migrant detention centre.

After a few days resting, the following week I was already studying English full-time, meeting people of different cultures and also learning the Australian culture, an interesting experience indeed. Four months later I found a job and continued studying English at night. A number of years later, I completed my studies as a tradesman landscaper and completed my diploma in Horticulture sciences. I am currently working in this field and enjoying my career as well.

The civil war finished after nine years of bloody fighting. Both parties reached an agreement but the country was destroyed, society divided and nothing was achieved. Today the country is slowly making some progress. In closing, I would like to express my sincere gratitude to the Australian government for giving me this window of opportunity, a new chance in my life taking me as a resident from that refugee camp of hell. A special thanks to my wife and two children who encouraged me to write this story which I did with so much pleasure and a heart full of gratitude.

my comments were handed to the planetary, which happened as it appeared. This was a midnight flight, a trip of thirteen hours when we landed at [illegible] my bag and joined the [illegible] procedure.

As I waited in line the other passengers went through with a [illegible] customs officer called [illegible] asked for my [illegible] I showed him my [illegible] and he [illegible] [illegible]

www.ingramcontent.com/pod-product-compliance
Ingram Content Group UK Ltd.
Pitfield, Milton Keynes, MK11 3LW, UK
UKHW020128250726
13967UKWH00002B/542